Lighthouse Mystery #6

KEY TO MURDER

By

TIM MYERS

Key to Murder
By Tim Myers.

Copyright © 2010 Tim Myers

All rights reserved.

For Patty and Emily

Chapter 1

There was a storm brewing at the lighthouse on the edge of the Atlantic Ocean, but it wasn't coming from the sea. Murder was in the air, something that seemed to follow Alex Winston wherever he went. This time though, he was eight hours away from home and nearly everything that was familiar to him.

Alex didn't realize it yet, but struggling to solve this murder would change his life forever in a way that he couldn't begin to fathom.

And those very same troubling times would lead him to the most desperate act he'd ever committed in his life.

Chapter 2

"I can't believe we're actually here," Elise Danton said to Alex Winston as they watched the sun rise out of the Atlantic through a break in the dunes. Elise and Alex worked together, but more importantly, at least to him, she was the one person he could ever imagine spending the rest of his life with. Alex kept that fact to himself, though. Elise had gone through a long engagement that had not ended well, and he knew that the last thing he should do was press her. For now, he was biding his time, happy that at last they'd found a way to come together; however much time they had, Alex was determined to cherish every last second of it.

He glanced over at Elise, taking in yet again how truly lovely she was, as they sat on the back porch of the inn at the Cape Kidd lighthouse on the coast of the Outer Banks of North Carolina. Her lustrous brunette hair was pulled back into the ponytail she often wore, and her jeans and simple top failed to do her justice.

This coastal lighthouse was a far cry from their regular place of business, even though they happened to work at a lighthouse themselves, though it was a long, long way from the nearest ocean. Alex, and his forefathers before him, owned Hatteras West, a replica of the Cape Hatteras Lighthouse nestled in the foothills of the Blue Ridge Mountains.

"I just hope Harry and Barbara are enjoying our lighthouse half as much as we are enjoying theirs. Alex, I admit that I wasn't sure about this at first, but I've got to admit that it was a great idea trading inns for a few weeks."

Alex smiled at Elise as he reached out to hold her hand. They'd been dating for nearly a year, and he still couldn't believe his good fortune. From the moment

Elise had first walked into the inn back in Elkton Falls
looking for a job, he'd known that she was the one for
him. He hadn't known that she'd be more qualified to
run his inn than he was. Her cousin, Marisa, had
worked for Alex at Hatteras West, but she'd suddenly
quit when the first dead body showed up at the top of
the lighthouse. Elise had handled it all like a seasoned
pro, though, and she'd often joined him on his
investigations of murder that followed. Once upon a
time, Alex had worried that working together at the inn
and dating would cause too much strain on their
relationship, but they'd somehow managed to balance it
all just fine.

"They must be in absolute heaven being in the
mountains," Elise said wistfully as the constant breeze
whipped a few strands of her hair around her face. The
salted sea air had a tang to it that wasn't necessarily
unpleasant, just unusual. Alex honestly preferred the
scent of honeysuckle. "As pretty as this place is, I have
to admit that I like ours better. I can't believe I'm
saying it, but I'm already getting homesick for our
lighthouse."

Alex loved how she referred to Hatteras West as
theirs. In his heart, he knew that it was because it was
true on so many levels. "I know exactly what you
mean. Lighthouses look almost out of place without
majestic mountains surrounding them, don't they?"

Elise laughed, a sound that he'd grown to love since
they'd first met. "That's it exactly. I've been trying to
put my finger on what's been so unsettling about the
place, but you're right. Every lighthouse should have
mountains."

Alex glanced at his watch, and then he reluctantly
released Elise's hand. "We'd better get back inside.
Don't forget. Mor and Emma are checking out today."

"An innkeeper's life is never an idle one, is it?"
Elise asked. "I'm going to hate to see the two of them

go." Mor Pendleton and his wife, Emma Sturbridge Pendleton, were Alex and Elise's closest friends. Mor was co-owner of Mor or Les, a fix-it shop in Elkton Falls, and Emma helped out sometimes at the inn when things got particularly hectic. She'd originally been hired to search for more precious stones on their property, but so far, the quest hadn't yielded many results. Their friends had taken a few days off from their lives in Elkton Falls to visit their friends at the coast, despite Les's protests, but they were heading back home today.

As if on cue, the screen door opened behind them. Alex was expecting to see his old friends, but instead, a couple in their late twenties joined them outside. They were both blond, dressed nicely in slacks and polo shirts, and were a little too pretty for Alex's taste. The man asked, "Nobody was out front at the main desk. I assume you two are part of the staff. Are you open yet?"

Alex stood, and Elise joined him. "As a matter of fact, we are. Do you have a reservation, by any chance?" He already knew that they didn't. It was slow during the offseason—one of the reasons Harry and his wife had suggested the inn swap—and there was no one scheduled to visit the inn until the weekend. Harry had told him that it was unusual to have drop-in guests this time of year, but it did happen, so it wasn't completely unexpected. They certainly had plenty of room for them.

"We were hoping you had space for us," the man said severely. "Judging by your parking lot, I'm guessing we were right."

My oh my, wasn't he a smug little twit? Alex was about to say something he'd most likely regret when Elise cut him off before he could say a word. "Of course there's space available. Let's go inside and get you checked in."

The four of them walked inside and made their way through the narrow hallway out into the main lobby where the front desk was located. Instead of the replica of the Hatteras Lighthouse's Main Keeper's Quarters they were used to, the Cape Kidd quarters were a little on the small size. Quaint little guest cottages had been built along the dune in the fifties, and it was a miracle they hadn't all washed away in one of the storms that occasionally hit the Outer Banks. Harry had told Alex that he was lucky to have an inland lighthouse inn and didn't have to constantly worry about beach erosion, but Alex had assured him that he had his own problems.

Alex put the guest ledger out on the counter of the scarred old oak desk. "If you'll just sign in, we can get you processed and assign you to one of our cozy cottages."

The man looked at him skeptically. "You *do* own a computer, don't you? I trust you at least have a way to handle a credit card. I'm afraid I don't usually carry much cash on me."

"Don't worry, we're able to accommodate you," Alex said. "The inn owners just like to keep a personal log of who visits them."

The woman looked surprised upon hearing the news. "Do you mean to say that you two aren't the owners? I assumed you were a married couple running your own operation. The place has a distinct mom-and-pop feel to it. No offense intended."

"None taken. We don't run this place, but we do operate another inn together in the mountains," Alex said.

"And we're not married, either, just to set the record straight," Elise chimed in.

"No, of course not," Alex hastily explained. "I mean, not of course, but it just so happens that we're not. We *are* dating, though. For about a year now." *Just shut up*, Alex chided himself. He couldn't believe that he still got flustered in these situations. The truth of the matter was that he'd thought about asking Elise to marry him more than once, but he didn't want to risk disturbing the delicate balance they'd found. If he asked her, and for some reason she said no, he was afraid that would be the end of them, both personally and professionally, and that was something he just wasn't willing to risk.

The woman smiled at his blushing cheeks and his stammering response. "Sorry, I didn't mean to touch a nerve. By the way, I'm Michelle, and this is Jackson. We're the Bennings." She said the last bit with a special trill, and Alex wondered if they were newlyweds.

"We're pleased to meet you," Elise said.

Alex nodded. As Jackson slid his credit card across the counter, Alex asked, "May I see your driver's license?"

Jackson looked peeved for just a second, but then he reluctantly complied. Alex felt that he should explain himself. "We don't ask for identification at Hatteras West, but the owners asked me to confirm IDs while we're here, so we're simply complying with their request."

"That's perfectly fine," Michelle said. "If you could manage it, we'd really like something private."

"I could put you in one of the end cottages," Alex said. "It's called the Seafarer. How long will you be with us here at the Hat...Cape Kidd?"

"We might be here for as long as a week, but I'd rather handle it one night at a time," Jackson said. "Is that going to be a problem?"

"No problem at all, but I can offer you a better rate if you do decide to stay with us a week," Alex said.

The man looked amused by Alex's offer. "Thanks for the suggestion, but cost is not going to be an issue for us."

Alex shrugged without commenting as he opened

the top of the desk, showing a modern station complete with computer and printer. He didn't know who had modified the desk, but he wished he had one himself. After running the card through the reader, a bill printed out, and he handed Jackson a copy to sign. After the task was completed, Elise handed them a key.

"I thought you said you didn't have a computer," Jackson said in an accusing voice.

"No, sir. It was your assumption. I just didn't correct you."

He didn't look at all pleased with Alex's response. "Is someone available to get our bags?" Jackson asked a little petulantly.

"I'll be more than happy to take care of that for you myself," Alex replied.

Michelle smiled at his response. "I like a man who can accomplish multiple tasks. Tell me something, Alex. Is there anything you *don't* do around here?"

"Well, I don't cook," he admitted. "Elise is the chef." Alex kept the fact that he baked the bread to himself. Somehow it felt as though he was showing off, trying to impress her because of her husband's dismissive attitude. The truth was, there was only one woman he cared about impressing.

"Hey, don't forget, I'm the head of housekeeping, too," Elise added with a smile. "We both believe in handling anything that comes our way, and so far, we've been a pretty successful team doing it."

Alex wasn't about to dispute it. In fact, he liked being thought of as part of a team, especially when it included Elise.

"That's excellent," Michelle said.

As Alex followed them out to their car, he glanced back at Elise and raised one eyebrow in question. She shrugged and added a gentle smile as he left. They'd just spoken paragraphs without saying a word. He'd wanted to know what she thought of their new guests, and she had said that, while she was hopeful, she wasn't ready to commit just yet to an opinion about them one way or the other.

Alex was expecting a great deal of luggage when they opened the trunk of their late-model Mercedes, but instead, he discovered that the space held just two slim overnight bags. Why did the man need help with these? It wasn't Alex's place to question the request as an innkeeper, but it did make him wonder. Alex dutifully grabbed both bags, and then he walked them to their cottage. When they all got there, he asked Michelle for the key, and then he unlocked the door. It was a quaint little space, with a double bed, an easy chair, a small pine dresser, and a tiny bathroom not much bigger than a closet. There were nautical themes present everywhere, from paintings showing ships in storms to seashell-filled glass lamps on each of the small nightstands. The bed was covered with a faded yellow spread that looked older than Alex, and the scarred wooden floors had gaps between the boards. A painted cast iron lighthouse nearly two feet tall sat in the corner, and Alex always smiled when he saw it. How could he not? After all, it was a replica of the Cape Hatteras lighthouse, in a small way just like his own was. Harry must have gotten a deal on the cast iron pieces, since there was one in each of the cottages.

"Is this all there is to it?" Jackson asked as he looked around the modest room in obvious distaste. "I'm assuming from what we see that there's not another room attached."

"No, this is it. What you see is what you get," Alex said without apology.

"Don't you have anything larger?" Jackson asked stubbornly, clearly not happy with the innkeeper's response.

"No, sir, I'm afraid not," Alex replied with a pursed smile.

Michelle smiled. "Don't be such a poo, Jackson. This cottage is fine. In fact, it's rather cozy, isn't it?"

"I suppose," Jackson replied grumpily.

It was time for Alex to leave before he said something that he might regret. After all, this income would go to Harry and Barbara, so it wasn't fair of him to risk it. He put the luggage on the bed and left the key on the small dresser. "We serve breakfast every morning, and if you'd like to have dinner with us, we need to know in advance. Breakfast is complimentary, but there is a modest fee for the evening meal. If you'd like, sandwiches are sometimes available for lunch if you feel like having a picnic while you're staying here with us. I believe Elise said that we were having egg salad sandwiches for lunch."

"We'd like lunch and dinner, please," Michelle said. "No breakfast. I don't know how anyone can eat early in the morning."

"Coffee, perhaps?" Alex suggested.

"Yes, that would be nice," Michelle agreed.

"Could we have it delivered promptly at nine tomorrow? I assume that you at least offer room service?" Jackson asked, though Alex suspected he already knew the answer.

"I'm afraid not," Alex said. "As a matter of fact, we're a little short-handed around here this time of year. Tell you what. We'll provide today's lunch on the house. You can pick up your sandwiches around noon, and dinner is served promptly at six."

"That early? Does anyone actually eat then?"

"You might be surprised," Alex said.

"We need to live like the locals, Jackson," Michelle said.

His only answer was a shrug. Clearly Alex wasn't the only one in the room who didn't trust himself to speak.

As Alex headed for the door, Michelle urged her

husband, "Tip him, Jackson."

Jackson started to reach for his wallet when Alex said, "I appreciate the sentiment, but it won't be necessary." He felt it wasn't appropriate for the proprietor to get tips at Hatteras West, and he saw no reason to change that policy while he was working on the coast.

"Don't be difficult. We insist," Michelle said, pouting a little.

Jackson pulled out a twenty and slid it into Alex's hand. It was clear that he wasn't about to be dissuaded, so there was no sense protesting. After all, he didn't have to be rude about it. It wasn't as though the thought of having a little extra money offended him.

Chapter 3

When Alex walked back into the main quarters of the inn, Elise was standing at the desk waiting for him. He loved the way the light hit her beautiful dark hair and how her smile seemed to light up any room she was in. There were no two ways about it; Alex was smitten, totally and completely, though he honestly believed that he hid it well.

Little did he know how wrong he was.

"Mor and Emma are out for a last stroll on the beach before they leave," Elise said.

"Did I miss them?" Alex had hoped to at least have the opportunity to say good-bye to his friends.

"No, I found a note tacked up in the kitchen. So tell me, what did our new guests have to say?" Elise asked.

"Not a lot that wasn't pretty condescending."

"How about the food situation?" she asked, always the practical one.

"They want egg salad sandwiches for lunch, and they're having dinner with us, even if it's at six, which they clearly found barbaric. I offered them their sandwiches on the house, as long as they came by and got them themselves. Can you believe it? He actually gave me a tip," Alex said with a smile as he held the twenty-dollar bill up.

"Alex Winston," she said. "What happened to your ironclad policy about not accepting gratuities from paying guests?"

"Hey, I tried to decline, but they insisted. What was I going to say?"

"Maybe we can use it to go out for some seafood before we go back home," she said. "I know you're allergic, but every place I've seen has burgers on the menu too, and I know for a fact that you're not allergic to them."

"That sounds perfect. I'm just sorry that it can't be tonight, since the Bennings will be joining us for dinner. They wanted room service, if you can believe that."

"From them? I have no trouble accepting that whatsoever. Let's see, what should I make tonight?"

"You're the chef. It's your call," Alex said.

Elise frowned in concentration for a moment before she said, "The larder's getting kind of low. We should do a little shopping soon."

"Just make me out a list and I'll take care of it myself," Alex said. As he spoke, the door opened, and a single man walked in. He was in his late forties and sported a mustache that had more pepper than salt in it, but not by much. He was handsome, in a dark sort of way.

"May I help you?" Elise asked.

He seemed to take her in for a moment as a prolonged instant of uncomfortable silence passed between them. Alex was certain that he was about to make a comment to Elise about her being beautiful, but a frown leapt instantly to her face, and he astutely changed his mind at the last second. Elise may have been a beauty queen once upon a time, but she wasn't all that comfortable dealing with her extraordinary good looks.

"I'd like a room," the man said simply.

"How many nights?" Alex asked.

"One to start."

Alex pointed to the sign-in book. "Just sign in there and we'll get you settled."

The man hesitated for an instant, but then Alex saw him scribble something down. From where he stood, it was entirely illegible.

After Alex quoted him the reduced off-season nightly rate, their new guest slid three hundreds across the desk. Alex started to give him his change, but the man said, "Keep whatever's left over," as he held out his hand for his key.

It may have been the largest tip he'd ever gotten in his life, but there were still matters that needed to be settled before he just handed over a room key. "I'm sorry, but I'll still need a credit card imprint for any additional charges that might accrue during your stay," Alex said. Though it was technically true, Alex was asking for another reason. He had a sudden desire to know this man's real name.

Instead of producing the requested card, the man offered him another hundred-dollar bill. "That should take care of any excesses. Now, if you'll give me a key, I'll be on my way."

Alex felt himself wavering. After all, it wasn't his money he'd be giving back if the man was adamant about not providing any identification, and he didn't feel as though the man was a particular risk to trash his room. He glanced over at Elise, who was not happy with the situation, either. That decided him.

"I'm sorry," Alex said as he reluctantly shoved the money back toward the guest. "I'm sure there are plenty of other places that would be more than happy to accommodate you. Unfortunately, we aren't going to be able to."

The man looked as though he was about to explode, but after a moment, he got his temper back in check. "If I provide you with a credit card, can I have your guarantee that no one will know that I'm here? Strict confidentiality is imperative."

"Is there something we need to know?" Elise asked softly over his shoulder.

"I'm not wanted by the law or anything like that. I have my reasons to be incognito, and I need your word that you won't disclose anything about me."

Elise shrugged, and Alex decided that he could do as he was asked. After all, being an innkeeper, it was a rare month that he didn't have at least one odd request.

"We can do that, right, Elise?"

"Of course," she answered.

The man handed over his card, albeit reluctantly, and Alex scanned it into his computer and tagged it to the cottage where the man would be staying. Why had he been so reluctant to provide it? It had simply said Marsh Enterprises on it. Who would know what that meant?

"I'll be glad to get your bags for you, Mr. Marsh," Alex said as he grabbed a key to the Whaler, the room farthest from his new guests as he could manage, all the way on the other side of the small lighthouse.

"No problem. I can handle it myself," he said as he grabbed the key.

Before he left though, Alex made one last stab at learning more about their guest. He looked at the book and said, "I'm having trouble making your signature out. Should we call you Mr. Marsh, or do you have a first name you'd like us to use?"

The man said, "Actually, the name is Brown," and then he left.

After Mr. Brown departed, Elise asked, "What do you suppose that was all about?"

"I wish I knew. I thought Harry said this was their slow time of year."

"Maybe it is normally, but it surely doesn't feel that way to me at the moment. What do you make of him?"

"Well, first off, I'm guessing Brown isn't his real name, and I doubt it's Marsh, either," Alex said. He was about to add something else when Mor and Emma walked in.

They were both frowning, and Alex had an immediate sense that something was wrong with his friends.

What had happened now?

Mor Pendleton was a big man, with thick, meaty hands and a football player's physique. Emma was no small woman, and together, they were a physical presence to be reckoned with. "What's up, you two?" Alex asked. "We were beginning to worry about you. How was your walk?"

"Unproductive. We were trying to hash something out, but we walked for hours, and it didn't do us the least bit of good."

"What's going on?" Elise asked them.

"The truth of the matter is that I want to stay," Emma said, "but Mor needs to get back to the shop."

"Hey, I'd love to hang around myself, but Lester is having a fit," Mor explained. "I pushed him as it was for us to even come here in the first place."

"I'm not ready to go," Emma said defiantly.

"Then stay," Mor said. There wasn't an ounce of harshness in his voice, but Alex was still a little unsettled every time he heard his friend and his wife discuss anything. There always seemed to be a bite to their words, whether they realized it or not.

"Not without you," Emma said.

Mor grinned. "What the matter, don't you trust me being on my own in Elkton Falls without you to supervise me?"

"You I trust," Emma said. "However, Molly Graves is a different story."

Alex knew that ever since Molly had moved to Elkton Falls, Emma had been suspicious of her overt affection for her husband. Alex knew that his friend's devotion to his wife was unwavering, and he was certain that she did as well, but Mor had a bad habit of tweaking his wife about the attention he got from other women, even though his life would have been easier if he didn't.

"I keep telling you, Emma, it's all in your imagination," Mor said.

"Maybe not all of it," Elise said softly. Alex wasn't even certain that she'd meant to say it aloud, but Emma jumped all over it.

"There, you see? It's not just me," she said accusingly. "That hussy has her sights set on you!"

Mor shook his head. "That's utter nonsense, and you know it. Come on, Elise, don't tell me you're buying it, too."

Elise shrugged. "I'm not sure, Mor. She does seem to have a great many things that are in need of repair."

"It happens, and Molly brings her business to us. That's what Les and I do; we fix stuff. It's all harmless."

Elise didn't look as though she agreed at all, and neither did Emma. Alex's friend finally appealed to him as he asked, "Surely you're on my side of this, right, buddy?"

"I don't have an opinion on the matter one way or another," Alex said in a level voice. Just because Mor was in the fire pit, that didn't mean that Alex was ready to jump in beside him, especially when Alex thought the women were right.

"Coward," Mor told him with a smile.

"I think he's smart," Emma said.

"You would. So, are you coming with me, or not, woman?" In a softer voice, he added, "I want you with me, Emma. Here or there, it doesn't matter, as long as we're together."

His wife seemed to debate it for a moment, and then she finally said, "I'd better go back home with you, then. After all, *somebody's* got to keep an eye on you." She hugged her husband fiercely as she said it, and then she followed it up with a kiss.

Mor's grin beamed once he broke free. "I'm glad. To be honest with you, I miss you when you're not around."

"That's sweet of you to say," Emma said, and then

she turned to Alex and Elise. "We're so sorry that we have to go. We love being here with you both."

"It's been great having you, but we understand that you need to get back," Elise said.

Alex added, "Do me a favor when you get home, would you? Pop in at the lighthouse and see how things are going there."

Emma raised an eyebrow. "Alex Winston, are you seriously asking me to check up on your friends?"

Alex shook his head. "No, it's nothing like that. I just want to make sure they're doing okay. It's not like I'm the only one doing it. Where did you think I got the idea? Harry's best friend, Slick, has been over here twice since we got here, so it's not like he won't be expecting me to return the favor. After all, if you look at it one way, it's just the neighborly thing to do."

Mor nodded. "No worries. We'll drop by tonight on our way to the cottage." He glanced at his wife, and then he added, "That is if we, by some miracle, ever happen to get on the road by noon."

Emma glanced at her watch and shook her head. "We could have left half an hour ago if you hadn't wanted to look for more seashells on our last walk, as if we didn't have a trunk full of them already."

Mor seemed embarrassed by the revelation of what they'd been up to since they'd come for their visit. The news delighted Alex, since it gave him something brand new to tease his best friend about when they saw each other again.

Mor explained, "You know they aren't for me, they're for Lester. He loves 'em, for some reason."

"Tell him that he can come himself, if he'd like to," Elise said. "We've got plenty of room."

"At least at the moment, anyway," Alex explained, "but the way things are going, that might not be true soon."

"Are things starting to pick up?" Mor asked.

"I just hope Harry and Barbara are as busy as we're about to be," Alex said.

After they shared hugs all the way around—even a brief one between Mor and Alex—the married couple took off to return to the mountains.

As Alex and Elise watched them drive away, he asked her softly, "Is there any part of you that wishes we were going with them?"

"I won't deny that I miss Hatteras West," she admitted, "but if it's all the same to you, I'll stay right here with you."

"I can't tell you how happy I am to hear that," Alex said as he put an arm around her, and he was delighted when she returned the gesture.

"Because you'd miss me too much?" she asked him with a smile.

"Of course there's always that, but another reason is that my cooking would probably run all of our guests off, so there wouldn't be any reason for either one of us to stay then."

Elise laughed and hugged him a little tighter. "You've got a point, there."

They were just about to go back inside when a large black SUV drove down the crushed-shell drive toward them.

It appeared that their stream of unexpected visitors wasn't quite over yet.

It meant a healthy income for the absent inn owners, but for Alex and Elise, all it meant was more work, on what had been proposed as a working vacation.

Apparently there would be more work than vacation if this kept up.

Chapter 4

"Who could this be?" Elise asked. "We're not expecting anyone else until the weekend, are we?"

"Not according to our reservation list," Alex replied. "If this keeps up, we're going to have to move Dutch back into his old shack." Dutch, first name only, was the part-time handyman who lived at Cape Kidd full time the year round. Harry had told Alex that in exchange for doing the occasional odd job around the place, Dutch stayed in a small building of marginal disrepair that was really not much more than a gardener's shed.

"Let's hope not," Elise said. "I don't have the heart to evict him from the cottage."

"I'm not sure I do either," Alex said.

Three adults somewhere in their forties got out of the SUV, though it could have held twice as many people.

The two men wore fashionable clothing, slacks and nice shirts. They stretched near their vehicle as though they'd been driving for some time while the stylish woman in a navy-blue suit of her own approached them. "We're the Morrisons, and I must say, we didn't expect a welcoming committee," she said.

"If we knew you were checking in, we might have planned it," Alex admitted.

She turned to one of the men and called out, "John. They didn't know we were coming. Explain to me what's happening."

"I'm not sure what I can tell you, Elizabeth. All I know is that I made our reservations for the tenth," John said.

"That's all well and good, but today is the ninth," Alex replied gently. "Not that the date really matters, since you don't have reservations here for either date anyway."

"John, come here please," she called out, and the man she'd been speaking with approached the group.

When he neared them, Elizabeth said, "The innkeeper just told me that we don't have reservations here at all."

John frowned. "This is the Kidd Motel, correct?"

Alex shook his head. "Sorry, it's the Cape Kidd Lighthouse Inn. The place you are looking for is on the other side of town. Go back down to Main and turn right, then keep going until you hit the city limit sign."

Elizabeth looked around. "I like it here."

"So do we," Alex answered.

"Then we'll stay. You do have room for us, don't you?"

"We've got space available," Elise said.

"Three individual rooms, I trust?" the woman asked.

"Better than that," Alex replied. "We have three individual cottages open, if you'd like them." It would leave them with no spare rooms for the next few days, but that wouldn't be an issue. There wasn't an innkeeper alive who didn't dream about having every bed booked. "Why don't we get you signed in?"

Elizabeth looked at the two men before she'd budge. "Greg, why don't you stay with the car? John, perhaps you should keep him company." Though it had been worded as a request, there was no doubt in Alex's mind that it had been a firm order, and what was more, the men knew it.

John didn't look pleased by the command, but Greg seemed delighted. Alex got the impression that the farther away he could be from Elizabeth, the better. What an odd dynamic they had going. Elizabeth must have had some kind of power over them both, because neither one clearly ever even considered going against her wishes.

Without looking back to see that her order had been followed, Elizabeth walked into the keeper's quarters, with Alex and Elise trailing her. Alex was about to say something when the woman stopped him at the door and asked, "Are you two coming in as well?"

"Yes, ma'am," Alex said. "We're going to have to, since we're the only two employees currently on the grounds."

"Very good," she said, as if her approval mattered one way or the other.

As Elizabeth checked the three of them in with her credit card, she remarked, "I'm glad we were able to beat the storm here."

"What storm are you talking about?" Alex asked. He had been so busy dealing with his friends leaving and the rush of unexpected guests that he'd foregone checking the weather report. Harry had insisted that he needed to tune in frequently because of changing weather patterns on the coast, but he'd forgotten all about it. Was his negligence going to turn around and bite him?

"You haven't heard? There's a tropical storm moving up the coast. It was supposed to head out to sea, but the winds shifted suddenly, and now it's heading straight for us tonight. I thought you people would be a little savvier about watching the weather out here, isolated as you are."

"The truth is, we normally live in the mountains," Alex admitted. "We swapped inns with friends of ours, so this is all new to us."

"Apparently they picked an excellent time to leave," Elizabeth said.

Elise asked tentatively, "Is it supposed to be that bad?"

"Who knows? From what I understand, these things have a tendency to blow themselves out. Would we have come to the coast if we thought we were in any danger?"

Alex didn't know what they might do, but he promised himself to turn on the radio and check for forecasts once his guests were all situated. They didn't have a television at the inn, Harry had explained, not even in the two small rooms in the main keeper's quarters where he and Elise were staying. Their guests liked to get away from the world, something that was impossible with around-the-clock access. Alex hadn't missed it until now, what with all of the natural beauty of the ocean being just a few footsteps away, but he was beginning to realize just how isolated they really were.

At least they had paying guests, though, even if that meant more responsibility for them as innkeepers.

In fact, it appeared that the Cape Kidd inn was going to be nearly full. With that and a possible storm coming inland, it was all going to be a little too exciting for Alex's taste.

So much for the quiet and restful vacation he and Elise had been hoping for.

"Alex, these people are impossible," Elise said as she burst into the dining room of the main keeper's quarters, where he was setting the tables. It was nearing six, and they were going to be so full that he and Elise might have to eat in the kitchen. That was, if he even got to sit down to eat. Alex would join her if he could, but he'd be serving dinner and waiting on their guests. That was one reason he liked the fact that they just served breakfast at the Hatteras West. Elise had been steadily pushing him about offering a dinner menu for nearly a year, but the only way Alex would agree to that was if they hired a couple of kids from a nearby college to wait tables. He wore many hats in his job as owner of Hatteras West, but being a waiter/busboy was not a title he cared to add to his resumé.

"You know as well as I do that guests can be a little

demanding at the best of times," Alex said as he paused in setting tables. The inn was quite different from Hatteras West, in that it offered a full kitchen and an expansive dining room as well, though the space that had been sacrificed to make it happen had been taken from the two small bedrooms where Alex and Elise were currently staying. At least the lobby was on the large side, big enough to support several couches and chairs, the check-in desk, and a rather large fireplace on the wall opposite the ocean view. "Whatever it is, we're just going to have to swallow it and smile."

"I understand that," Elise said, a rare burst of irritation radiating from her. "But the Bennings are suddenly insisting that we offer them a vegetarian menu. I tried to explain that I didn't have much on hand in the way of supplies and that the pending storm has probably wiped out the store shelves even if we did have the time to go shopping, but they wouldn't listen."

"What are you planning on serving the rest of us?" Alex asked, his curiosity getting the better of him.

"I made beef stew for the main course tonight, and we can have some of the homemade bread you made yesterday to go with it. There should at least be plenty of that. It was the best I could do, given the supplies on hand."

Alex loved Elise's cooking, and his mouth instantly began to water thinking about the prospect of grabbing a bowl of stew for himself. Maybe he'd sneak his meal in before they started serving their guests. At least that way he wouldn't be tempted to taste everyone else's order. "They could always pick out the meat," Alex said.

"Clearly you don't know any vegetarians. It's a legitimate lifestyle choice, and I respect it, but I wasn't prepared for the request. Even if I could remove the meat, which wouldn't do any good at all; what about the liquid? It's beef broth, Alex, and it's infused in everything. I'll do my best to come up with *something* for them, but you need to warn them that I'm working with hands tied behind my back given the state of our larder."

Alex nodded. He'd dealt with his share of demanding customers in the past, and it wasn't anything he couldn't handle. "I'll tell them the moment I see them, but in the meantime, can I eat before I have to serve everyone else? You know how grumpy I get if I don't get my meals on time."

Elise patted his cheek and smiled gently. "Don't worry. I've got a bowl ready for you in the kitchen," she said.

Alex nodded, and then, as Elise returned to the kitchen, he walked out of the dining room and into the lobby. The Bennings were the only ones there, and Jackson was not at all pleased, though he could swear that Michelle looked amused by all of the fuss.

"May I help you?" Alex asked.

"I certainly hope so. We need two vegetarian meals," Jackson said, "and your cook seemed uncooperative in accommodating us. She should be terminated immediately for her blatant insolence."

"She wasn't insolent," Michelle said, trying to appease him.

It was all Alex could do not to laugh at the accusation. The idea that he'd fire Elise for any reason, let alone based on a trumped-up charge that he knew had to be false, was ridiculous. Alex did his best to keep his voice calm and level as he explained, "I'm sorry you feel that way, but special dietary requests need to be made one week prior to your stay. We have to stock the kitchen, after all." Alex didn't know if this was true or not, but it might be the best way to defuse the situation.

"Are you telling me that your chef can't make us *anything* at all to eat?" Michelle asked. "It doesn't have to be fancy. We aren't that choosy."

Alex was about to comply with her perfectly reasonable request when Jackson grabbed his wife's arm. "Forget it. Let's go. We'll eat somewhere else."

"Jackson, there's no reason to be that way," she said. "You heard what that woman said. There's a storm coming, and it might get bad. I'd rather eat here."

"You heard me, Michelle. We're leaving," he said.

She shot a look of apology to Alex, and then the two of them left.

Alex walked back in and saw that the dining room was still empty, so he headed for the kitchen and took in a deep breath of the glorious aroma of beef stew as he entered the room. As promised, Elise had set aside a bowl on the counter for him, along with a thick slab of his own homemade bread. Instead of bringing her up to date on his recent conversation, he headed straight for the food when she cut him off.

"What did they say?"

"The problem's solved," Alex answered as he looked around for a spoon. If he didn't find one fast, he was going to use the bread and sop up as much of the liquid goodness as he could manage, manners be hanged. He knew that he didn't have much time, so he wasn't going to waste it on formalities.

"How exactly did you solve it?"

"They're gone," Alex said simply as he kept looking around the kitchen. There was a ladle on the counter. Would that work? Probably not. "Is there a spoon around here I could use, or do I have to use my fingers?"

"You threw them out? Listen, I overreacted before. Go get them and bring them back."

Alex shook his head. "Not me. I know better than to try to restrain someone against their will. Elise, they left of their own accord."

"And now, because of me, they aren't even staying

at the inn? I could have whipped something up for them if they'd just asked me nicely."

"Relax. They aren't leaving, they're just going to get something to eat somewhere else, but they'll be back later," Alex replied. "Now, give me a spoon, or things are about to get messy."

Elise handed him a spoon, and he dug in. Alex couldn't believe how wonderful the simple meal was. He respected the Bennings' choice in what they consumed, but he knew that personally, he could never follow that particular path. He loved what he ate too much to give any of it up, though to be fair, his consumption of red meat and whole milk had been drastically reduced since Elise had come into his life, and the amount of vegetables he now ate had skyrocketed.

"Do me a favor. The next time you see them, tell them that I'll have something for them tomorrow," she said.

"If I see them first, I will be more than happy to," Alex promised between bites. "This is absolutely delicious. My compliments to the chef."

"Thanks, but the speed with which you're eating tells me that you're barely tasting it." He was nearly finished when Elise reminded him, "It's six o'clock, Alex."

"Another few minutes won't kill them," he said with a smile as he chased the last of the broth in the bottom of his bowl. "They can wait out in the hallway until I'm finished."

She took the spoon from him playfully and smiled. "Guess what? You're finished."

"At least save me some for later," Alex said as he washed his hands in the sink.

Elise laughed at the request. "Seriously? How can you still be hungry after eating all of that? You've had enough, don't you think?"

"Not even close." He leaned in and kissed her, something he doubted he'd ever grow tired of doing. "You're pretty wonderful; you know that, don't you?"

"That's what you keep telling me," Elise said. She swatted him lightly with her towel. "Now go. Our guests are waiting."

Alex saluted and added a smile and then put on his best server's expression. It was time to face his hungry guests.

He just hoped they appreciated their meals as much as he just had.

Chapter 5

To his surprise, the man named Brown was the only one waiting when Alex opened the door to the dining room at two minutes after six. He wore the same clothing he'd had on earlier, but his clothes were wrinkled, as though he'd taken a nap in them. At least part of his afternoon must have been spent sleeping, something Alex was envious of at the moment. As an innkeeper, sleep was one of the rarer commodities in his life.

Alex put on his best smile and said, "Feel free to sit wherever you'd like."

Brown nodded, and then he headed for the table farthest from the kitchen and facing the dining room door that led into the lobby. As he took the seat with his back to the wall, Alex walked over and joined him.

"Tonight we're having homemade beef stew, artisan bread, and banana pudding for dessert. Sorry we don't have more choices, but we weren't expecting anyone tonight, so we're running a lean menu until we can restock our pantry."

"Stew's fine," Brown said as he opened a newspaper that completely obscured his face, and he began to read. It was rude, but there was nothing Alex could do about it.

"Sweet tea to drink?" Alex asked. He didn't know much about the man named Brown, but from the drawl of his accent, it told him the man had been born somewhere in the South.

"Sure," Brown said, still not looking up from his paper.

Alex glanced out into the hallway as he headed for the kitchen, but no one else was out there yet. The handyman, Dutch, liked to eat with them in the kitchen,

and normally he was prompt when it came to getting fed
for free. Alex wondered where he was but then quickly
forgot about him the second he saw Elise standing at the
sink doing dishes, her lustrous dark hair pulled back in a
ponytail.

Alex saw that there were five waiting bowls on the
serving counter, one each for the three Morrisons, the
man named Brown, and the handyman, Dutch.
Evidently Elise had already eaten as well. She asked,
"Is everyone out there?"

"No, so far, it's just Brown. If you ask me, that man
talks too much. I could barely get a word in edgewise."

"Really? What did he say?" Elise asked, clearly
interested.

"Let's see. First he answered, 'Stew's fine' when I
told him what we were having, and then he said, 'sure'
when I asked him about having sweet tea to drink. The
man's practically a motor mouth. He's got his head
buried in a newspaper, and the way he's holding it, it's
hard to tell that he's even there."

"Is no one else going to eat tonight?" Elise asked as
she surveyed the large pot of stew simmering on the
stovetop.

"Give them time. I'm sure all three of the Morrisons
will be along shortly."

"What about Dutch?" she asked. "He's never been
late for a meal since we arrived."

"That I was wondering about myself. Should I go
look for him?"

"No," she replied. "I'm sure he'll find his way in as
soon as he gets hungry."

Alex grabbed the pitcher of sweet tea, and then he
put it on the tray with a bowl of beef stew and a thick
slab of the artisan bread he'd made himself. Elise loved
to cook, but Alex had really grown fond of baking
lately, especially bread. This loaf had a dark, crisp
crust, with a center that was filled with light and

flavorful goodness.

When he walked back into the dining room, he found the Morrisons standing impatiently by the door, as though they'd been waiting there for him for hours.

"Feel free to sit wherever you'd like," Alex said as he delivered the food to the mysterious Mr. Brown. He noticed that the man looked the three new guests over carefully before returning his attention to his paper. It was almost as though he was disappointed seeing them there.

Alex put the food down in front of Mr. Brown and then asked, "Will there be anything else, sir?"

"Just the check," Brown said. "I might have to leave in a hurry."

What an odd thing to say. Where would he go, with the growing bad weather approaching up the coast? Alex replied, "No worries on that account. We'll add it to your bill, and it will be deducted from that incidental hundred you left instead of your card, if you're okay with that."

"Good enough."

Alex shook his head slightly as he moved to the Morrisons. Working at Hatteras West had taught him that guests could be the oddest folks on earth, but Brown was setting the bar even higher than Alex had seen before.

Thankfully, the Morrisons were all happy with stew and homemade bread, and as he served them, Alex admired the way they dug in.

He was heading back to the kitchen for a quick word with Elise when he saw their handyman start to come in through the outside door. Of an almost indeterminate age, Dutch had a full beard and long brown hair pulled back into a ponytail. His clothes were most likely from Goodwill, but they were clean and in good repair, and his worn shoes had a shine to them. Dutch nodded to Alex, glanced into the room, and then left just as suddenly.

Alex was concerned about the expression he'd seen on the man's face before he'd vanished.

"Dutch, are you okay?" Alex asked as he caught up with him just outside.

"Didn't realize that we had any guests. I should have come in through the kitchen, but to be honest with you, I'm feeling a tad under the weather," Dutch said. "I felt a little queasy just then. I'm not sure I'm up for company tonight."

Well, he was certainly pale enough. "Some of Elise's stew is just what you need. At least get some of that before you go to your cottage."

"I hate to ask, but would you mind bringing me some?" Dutch asked plaintively. "I don't think I could make it to the kitchen and back."

"Sure, I can do that, but it might not be right away," Alex answered, not entirely sure that waiting on the handyman was part of his job description. But if the man was truly ill, which Alex didn't doubt, how could he say no? "I'll bring you some tea and bread, too."

"You're a life saver," Dutch said as he rushed out the door.

Since his guests were all eating, Alex realized that he had time to take care of the errand sooner rather than later. As Alex joined Elise, he told her, "I need one stew and all the trimmings to go."

"Alex, I promise you there will be enough left for you when we close the kitchen."

"It's not for me. Dutch is feeling a little under the weather, and he asked me to bring him something to the cottage. You don't mind, do you?"

"Of course not." A look of concern spread on Elise's face. "How terrible. Let me fix something up for him, and you can take it straight to him."

Alex watched as Elise gathered a little basket together, transferring some stew into a Tupperware container, adding a bottle filled with sweet tea, and a generous portion of Alex's bread. She frowned for a second and then added some wrapped silver and a vase with one of the flowers from the kitchen, a bouquet Alex had just bought for her the day before. "You don't mind me stealing one of your lovely flowers, do you?"

"Of course not," Alex said. He loved the nurturing side of her, and she'd taken good care of him during a bout he'd had with the flu a few months before. While Alex had felt like dying, hiding in his room for three straight days, Elise had managed to run the inn at Hatteras West mostly by herself, with just a little help from their friend, Emma.

Alex took the basket out, and then he glanced around the dining room. It appeared that no one even noticed him, but he wasn't even to the lobby door before the man Brown caught up with him and put a strong hand on his shoulder.

"Where are you taking that?" Brown asked, as though he was accusing Alex of doing something illicit.

"Our handyman's under the weather, so I'm taking him a care package," Alex explained. "Why do you ask?"

"No reason," Brown let him go as he replied, as though he were disappointed with the innkeeper's response.

This guy was seriously odd, and Alex vowed to keep an eye on him.

Once he was outside in the approaching dusk, he realized that it was beginning to rain, so Alex ducked back in and grabbed a raincoat, then he covered the basket with another one that Harry and Barbara provided to their guests. By the time he got back to the porch, it was already coming down in sheets. There was no way he was going to get himself soaked in the downpour. He was still standing on the porch waiting for a break in the rain when Michelle and Jackson drove up in their car, though they didn't get out.

"What's that?" Jackson asked as he rolled down his window to talk to Alex. "I didn't think you offered room service."

"We don't," Alex explained. "It's for our handyman. I'm taking him something to eat since he's under the weather."

"It looks like we all will be soon, the way it's pouring," Michelle said. "Please tell him that we hope he feels better soon."

Behind him, Alex heard one of the shutters come loose in the wind and bang against the side of the main quarters.

As he put the basket down on the porch and turned to latch the shutter back, Jackson drove away to their cottage, kicking up the crushed seashell that made up the drive as he sped off.

The rain didn't look like it was going to ease up anytime soon, so Alex decided it was time to make a dash for it anyway. He got to Dutch's cottage, soaked to the bone, and then he had to knock on the door three times before the man let him in.

"Sorry, I was in the bathroom."

"Feeling any better?"

"Not yet, but I bet I will be soon. I appreciate you waiting on me. I don't mean to be such a bother."

"No worries," Alex said as he put the basket down on the dresser. "It's really storming out there. Do you ever lose power here?"

"All of the time," Dutch said as he started digging into the basket. "There are candles in the kitchen, and don't forget about the fireplace in the main entry. It will keep you warm."

"I never thought about actually having a fire in the fireplace on the Outer Banks."

"Trust me, it gets plenty cold here in the winter," he said. "We even get snow sometimes. That's a sight to see, let me tell you."

"I don't suppose you have a generator," Alex said.

"Never saw the need for the expense," Dutch said. "The power's not the main problem we've got, anyway."

"What could be worse than losing your electricity?" Alex asked. He couldn't imagine stumbling around in the dark so close to the ocean.

"If the storm's bad enough, it could wash out the road. Then we're stuck here until someone comes along and digs us out of the sand. That is if they remember us at all."

Great. Harry had neglected to mention any of that when he'd first proposed the lighthouse swap, and Alex was beginning to wonder just who had gotten the better part of that particular deal. There was nothing he could do about it now though, other than do his best to weather the storm.

"Let me know if you need anything," Alex said as he headed back for the door.

"I'll be fine here," Dutch said. "I'm sure that I just need a good meal and a solid night's sleep. There's no need to worry about me."

Alex nodded, and then he wrapped himself in one of the rain jackets as he made his way back to the main quarters. At least he and Elise wouldn't have to brave the storm. There were two small, austere rooms in the central building, and they'd each taken one the day they'd arrived.

As Alex struggled through the growing wind and rain, he hoped his guests would be all right. It was the innkeeper in him that made him realize that no matter where he was, he always thought of his customers first.

As Alex got back to the main keeper's quarters, as predicted, he was soaking wet, despite the protective gear he'd worn.

Chapter 6

Alex was surprised to find the Morrisons standing on the front porch, looking out at the weather with great distaste.

"Is it going to let up soon?" Elizabeth asked.

"I'm no expert, but it doesn't look like it's going to to me," Alex said. "We've got raincoats for everyone, and if we lose power, there are candles in all of the cottages."

Elizabeth turned to John. "You said you wanted to see what the Outer Banks had to offer. It appears you're about to get your wish."

"Greg wanted to come here, too," John said.

"You're *both* disappointing to me, then," Elizabeth said, then she went inside, grabbed a rain-jacket, and then headed into the storm. The two men watched her go, and it appeared they'd forgotten all about Alex for a moment. John said, "You know, your sister is more than just a little bit crazy."

"Maybe so, but she's nowhere near as crazy as yours," Greg answered.

Both men laughed, and Alex said, "I'm sorry. I don't mean to be rude, but I don't get it."

John smiled ruefully at Alex. "It's an old family joke. Elizabeth is the oldest, and she's always been a little odd."

"And more than a little mean," Greg added. "And quite bossy, too."

"I couldn't have said it better myself, bro. Are you ready to get wet?"

"As I'll ever be." The men grabbed jackets themselves, and then they both took off into the growing night. At least the lights in front of each cottage were still lit, for now, anyway, so they could find their way.

Alex was surprised to see that Mr. Brown was back at his table, his head again buried in the paper. How had he found that much to read? It was nearing seven, and Alex was ready to close the dining room for the night. He ran a hand through his wet hair as he approached the last diner. When Alex glanced at Brown's bowl, he saw that the stew was gone, but the bread on his side plate hadn't been touched.

"Was there something wrong with that?" Alex asked as he pointed to the bread.

"I'm sure some people like it, but it's not to my taste," Brown said.

Alex shrugged. He wasn't about to confess that he'd made it himself. "We'll try to do better tomorrow. We're closing, so feel free to enjoy our lobby before you go, or you can always make your way back to your cottage."

Brown looked surprised by the announcement. "Has everyone who's staying here already eaten tonight?"

"There's just one other couple, but they ate out, so we're wrapping up for the night."

Brown looked outside as the wind blew the rain against the panes as though they were in a car wash. "They might not make it back in this mess."

"No worries. They're already here," Alex said. "Everyone is present and accounted for."

Brown nodded, and then he left the dining room without another word, leaving his newspaper behind.

Alex gathered up the dirty dishes, and then he headed into the kitchen.

"That's it," he said as he cleaned the bowls into the trashcan. "We're all clear."

"Our Mr. Brown finally left?"

"Not without a nudge from me," Alex answered.

She seemed to notice him for the first time. "Alex, you're soaking wet. Didn't you wear a raincoat?"

"As a matter of fact, I did, for all the good it did me.

It's getting nasty out there, and Dutch thinks we might lose power. He suggested we grab candles and light a fire in the fireplace."

"What a wonderful idea," Elise said. "I don't have much to do here. Why don't you go get into some dry clothes, and I'll meet you in the lobby. Barbara left me instructions to use the driftwood logs on the porch for our fire. She said sometimes they put off the most lovely colors when they've soaked in minerals from being in the ocean."

"Then let's go ahead and light the fire now." He looked around the kitchen. "These dishes can wait until tomorrow."

She threw a dishrag at him playfully. "You know I'll never be able to get to sleep if we just leave them. If you really want to help, I'll wait until you change."

"That sounds good to me. I'll be back in a second," Alex said. He quickly changed clothes in his room, and soon he rejoined her.

"That was fast," Elise said. "I'll wash, and you can dry."

"I hate to admit it, but that's the best offer I've had all day."

After the dishes were done and the kitchen was cleaned up, Alex looked around. "Hey, where's that stew you were saving me?"

"It's gone," Elise admitted. "You wouldn't believe how those Morrisons can eat! They had two servings each. I did save you some banana pudding, though."

Alex thought about it, and then he realized that he wasn't really all that hungry. "That's okay. It's not worth making another dirty dish."

Elise touched his face lightly. "You poor deprived man."

He took her in his arms and kissed her. "Are you talking about me? I'm not *that* deprived. Are you ready for that fire?"

"It sounds lovely," she answered. They often had a fire at Hatteras West when there was the slightest chill in the air, and it was one of Alex's favorite things about being with Elise. It felt as though they could really talk in those moments, sitting there staring at the dancing flames. He just hoped that she cherished the time as much as he did.

Alex lit the fire already laid up in the fireplace, but it took a few minutes to really catch. "We can add some driftwood later once it really gets going. My guess is that we're getting some backdraft from the storm," he said.

"It's going to be bad, isn't it?"

"Don't worry," Alex said as he retrieved some candles and put them firmly in their holders. "I'm sure that we'll be fine."

At that moment, the lights flickered once, twice, and then they went out completely.

It appeared that the storm was finally making its presence felt after all.

In the light of the flickering fire, Alex and Elise lit a handful of candles. Placed on the mantel, they gave off a soft glow reflected in the mirror that stood above it.

"That's really nice," Alex said as he settled back in on the couch.

Elise sat beside him and snuggled up close. "It's kind of cozy, isn't it? How wonderful to be safe and dry."

Alex nodded. "There's just one thing missing."

She leaned forward and turned to look at him. "What's that?"

"Banana pudding, and two spoons."

Elise laughed as she stood up suddenly. "I can fix that." She grabbed one of the candles, leaving the heavy candelabra on the mantel. "Don't you go anywhere, mister. I'll be right back."

She was as good as her word, and soon she returned with a decent-sized bowl and two spoons. "I saved this for us."

"I knew there was a reason I loved you," Alex said, marveling yet again how good it felt to be able to say it out loud.

"I hope you have more reasons than banana pudding," she answered with a smile.

"Let me see," he said, pretending to ponder her question. "Offhand, I can think of a couple of thousand," Alex replied. "Would you like to hear the list?"

"No, I trust you," she said. Before handing him a spoon, she gave him a quick kiss and said, "By the way, I love you, too."

"Because?" Alex asked.

She pinched his cheek playfully. "No fishing for compliments tonight. Just accept that it's true."

"I do," Alex said and then grabbed a spoon. "Let's eat."

Elise laughed. "I can always count on you to have dessert. A friend of mine used to say that if you can bake a cake, you can find a man."

"Banana pudding works, too," Alex said.

They chatted, enjoyed the fire and the pudding, and as the wood started to die down, Alex asked, "Should I put another log on the fire?"

"It's been a big day," Elise said as she yawned. "And we have to get up early to make breakfast. Would you mind if we call it a night?"

"I'm beat, too," Alex said. "Thanks again for coming here with me, Elise. I know it's been a lot of work, but it's been fun, too, hasn't it?"

She kissed him, long and lingering, and then said, "I wouldn't have missed it for the world. Good night, Alex."

"Good night," he answered. She took her candle

down the hall to her bedroom, and Alex used the iron poker to knock the remnants of the fire down. Elise was right in calling it a night. Tomorrow was another big day for them. Someday he hoped to take her on a real vacation where people waited on them and not a busman's holiday where they had to work, too. Not that Elise would ever complain about it, but Alex reveled in giving her the best experiences he could. She was so much a part of his life that he didn't know what he'd do without her.

As the storm continued to rage outside, he hoped that he never had to find out if he could manage on his own again.

Chapter 7

The next morning, Alex awoke to a gray haze outside his window. It appeared that the sun was trying to break free of the clouds, but it wasn't having a great deal of luck. At least the rain had stopped sometime in the night. There was a heavy quality to the air itself, as though it were gravid with moisture it was just waiting to release. Alex flicked the light switch off and on a few times and then realized that the power hadn't yet been restored to the inn.

He quickly dressed and made his way out into the lobby of the main quarters and then went into the kitchen. Elise was already up, putting a pan of biscuits into the oven. "Good morning, Alex. I'm thrilled they cook with gas here," she said. "I might have to mix everything by hand, but at least we'll eat. Did you sleep well?"

"I did. There's something about the salt air that just knocks me out."

"That's probably one of the main things I'll miss when we go back to Hatteras West."

"I know what you mean. We've got nearly a week left of our stay," Alex said. "I'm hoping we can take a few more walks on the beach before we go."

"I just wish we could turn the lighthouse lantern on again," Elise said. The lighthouse had been decommissioned for years, but Harry had gotten permission to light the old-fashioned kerosene lantern that hung free inside the lens on special occasions. Alex had misunderstood the instructions somehow, and he'd lit it the first two nights they'd been there. Their nearest neighbor, an old man with beady eyes and a stooped back, had stormed over to the inn, and he had declared that if Alex lit the lantern again before it was due in four weeks, he'd call the state police and have him thrown in jail. Alex didn't doubt the man would do just that, but he found himself wishing that he could see that beacon lit just once more before they left Cape Kidd behind for good. The exchange had been a great idea, but Alex doubted that he'd ever do it again. It was just too tough for him to be away from his own beloved lighthouse.

"We should call Tracy and see if we can light up Hatteras West when we get home," Alex said. "Now, that's a light." Tracy was the mayor of Elkton Falls and a good friend of Alex's going all the way back to kindergarten. She'd made sure once she'd been elected to get the town council to allow the lighthouse's illumination a great deal more than her predecessor had.

"I do miss it. Seeing Hatteras West's twin only made me more homesick," Elise said. The two of them had made a pilgrimage to the original lighthouse a few hours down the coast, and Alex had marveled at how close his ancestor had come to replicating it. Still, the one on the Outer Banks looked out of place to him. He agreed with Elise; the black-and-white-striped lighthouse on the coast made him homesick in a way that he never would have imagined was possible.

"Can I give you a hand with breakfast?" Alex asked, trying to shake the morose feelings he was having. Was the gloomy weather really having that much of an impact on his mood?

"Thanks for the offer, but I've got it covered. Why don't you take a walk and see if the storm caused any damage to the cottages?"

"That's a good idea," he replied. Alex stepped out on the porch, and he was immediately surprised by how much the temperature had dropped from the night before. The storm had not just brought rain; it had lowered the outdoor air temperature by a good fifteen degrees. Alex ducked back into his room for a sweater and a cap, and then he walked out again.

As he took in the view around him, the first thing he saw was the road leading into the inn.

Or more accurately, the lack of it.

Heavy sand, and lots of it, had been washed across it, leaving ridges and valleys that no car could traverse. To make matters worse, they were a good mile from the main road, and it would be a long hike through the terrain to even try to get help. For all intents and purposes, they were isolated. Alex feared that their situation was even direr than that. If the main road had taken a hit as bad as their drive had, it might be days before they were dug out of their sandy trap.

At least the exteriors of the cottages looked as though they'd stood up to the storm. Alex wasn't sure what the proper etiquette should be for knocking on individual doors, so he satisfied himself with looking around outside the buildings to see if he could spot anything wayward that might have happened during the night. The curtains were pulled shut in all three of the Morrison bungalows, as well as the small space Dutch occupied. Alex wondered if the handyman was feeling any better. Better let him sleep in, he thought.

At least the curtains to the Benning cottage were pulled aside, and as Alex walked by, the front door opened.

It was Michelle Benning, dressed in casual clothes and smiling brightly. "Good morning, Alex. It's lovely out today, isn't it?"

He took a deep breath, and then he agreed with her despite the oppressive texture of the air all around them and the heavy clouds permeating the sky. "If the weather holds, I'll be happier, but I have to admit that I love it here. It's going to be a little sad leaving it."

"That's right, your inn is in the mountains. Tell me, what's it like there?"

"Believe it or not, it has a lighthouse, too," Alex said with a grin.

Michelle clearly didn't believe him, something Alex was used to. She asked with a puzzled expression on her face, "Why would there be a lighthouse in the mountains? Is it some kind of miniature?"

"No, it's a full-sized replica of the Hatteras Lighthouse, all the way down to the diagonal stripes."

"I don't understand," she repeated.

"One of my ancestors was a hopeless romantic trying to appease his new bride's homesickness," Alex said. "She grew up here on the Outer Banks, but sickness made her too fragile to ever return, so he did the next best thing. If he couldn't bring his wife to the lighthouse, he decided to bring the lighthouse to her."

Michelle took the explanation at face value. "That I understand. A man in love can be a powerful force to reckon with."

"Where's Mr. Benning this morning?" Alex asked. He thought it was a natural segue, though after seeing her curious expression, he wasn't quite sure he had gotten that right.

"He's still asleep," she said. "We have completely different schedules. I love mornings, but I'm afraid that Jackson is more of a night owl. Would you care to take a short stroll with me along the water?"

Alex knew that he had a little time before breakfast, and Michelle Benning was pleasant company despite her husband's surly attitude. "Sure, that sounds great to me."

Alex and Michelle started walking down the beach together, chatting idly about the area as they went. They moved past a handful of the inn's cottages, paused to stare up at the lighthouse itself for a few moments, and then they made their way to the last cottage in the row, where something appeared to catch Michelle's eye. "Alex, should that door be open?"

Alex looked where she was pointing and saw that the door to the cottage where Mr. Brown was staying

48

was indeed ajar. He knew that he hadn't missed
something that obvious before, so it must have
happened since he'd inspected the cottage earlier.

"He must have just stepped out and forgot to close
it," Alex said as he neared the door. He knocked on the
doorframe and called inside, "Hello, Mr. Brown, is
everything okay? Are you there?"

There was no reply.

Alex knocked again, and when there was still no
response, he pushed the door open the rest of the way
and stepped inside.

Behind him, he heard Michelle Benning gasp as they
took in the scene.

At first it appeared that Mr. Brown was fast asleep
facedown on his bed, though he was still in his clothes
from the night before. But then Alex saw the blood on
the back of his head and the cast iron lighthouse on the
floor beside him, the base sporting a spattering of blood
and a small clump of hair.

Alex raced inside to the man to check for a pulse,
but the second his fingers hit Brown's neck, he knew
there was no use. The guest's skin was cold to the
touch, and there was no pulse that Alex could find.

He turned to tell Michelle that they were too late,
but she was already gone.

Almost as a matter of instinct, Alex pulled the door
shut, and then he locked it with the master key Harry
had given him to all of the cottages. He knew from past
experience that the police would want the crime scene
isolated, and there was nothing anyone could do for Mr.
Brown anymore. As he turned from the door, Michelle
Benning was dragging her husband toward the cottage
he'd just locked up.

As Jackson rubbed his eyes, he asked, "What's this
nonsense Michelle is spouting about the two of you
finding a body?"

"It's not nonsense," Alex said gravely. "One of our guests is dead."

Jackson shook his head as though he didn't believe it. "Are you certain about that? You're not a doctor. You could be wrong."

"He was clearly murdered. Someone hit him from behind with a cast iron lighthouse," Alex explained. "The body's cold to the touch, so my guess is that he's been dead for some time. There's nothing we can do for him." Alex pulled his cell phone out—something he'd been reluctant to buy but had quickly become attached to—and dialed 9-1-1. When he held the phone to his ear though, he got nothing.

His phone was completely incapable of picking up any signal whatsoever.

"Try your phone," Alex said. "I can't get through on mine."

Jackson pulled his phone from his pocket, checked it, and then he said, "I can't get any bars, either. The storm must have knocked out the towers around here."

"Maybe the landline will work," Alex said as he hurried back to the main quarters. Once he got there, he picked up the telephone, but as he'd feared, it was dead as well.

"So, that means that we're trapped here with a killer," Jackson said.

Michelle swatted him lightly as she replied, "Don't be so negative, Jackson. I'm sure Mr. Winston will be able to think of something."

Unfortunately, she was giving him entirely too much credit. "I'm afraid he's right," Alex said. "The drive is impassable, and even if we could make it past that, I'm afraid the main road is bound to be closed. Added to that, we don't have any way to call out. It looks like we're stuck until we're rescued."

"This is horrible," Michelle said, shocked when Alex had summed up their woes so succinctly. "What are we going to do?"

"You heard the man. There's nothing we can do," Jackson said. He must have smelled the biscuits Elise had been baking from where they stood. "Is that food I smell?"

"How can you think about eating at a time like this?" Michelle asked him.

"Michelle, there's nothing we can do for the man now," Jackson said. "And besides, we still have to eat."

"He's right," Alex agreed. "I'll go see when breakfast will be ready." At least they weren't vegan. Alex knew his guests ate eggs, since they'd taken the egg salad sandwiches Elise had made the day before.

The innkeeper walked into the kitchen to find Elise cooking a batch of scrambled eggs on the gas cooktop. She looked so natural there, so happy, that he felt miserable that he was about to ruin it.

Elise smiled at him the moment she saw him and said, "There you are. I thought you forgot all about me. What have you been up to?" Elise must have noticed his expression at that moment. "Alex? What's wrong? Did something happen?"

"I can't tell you how much I hate to tell you this, but I just found a body."

Elise dropped her spatula, and it clattered to the kitchen floor, sending bits of egg everywhere. "Oh, no. Was it washed up on the beach?"

"No, it was in one of our cottages. Mr. Brown is dead."

Elise shook her head. "I can't believe it. How did it happen? He looked so healthy yesterday."

Alex grabbed a clean spatula and stirred the eggs before they could burn. He wasn't sure how much food they had on hand or when they'd be able to get fresh supplies with the road closed, so it was imperative that they didn't waste any of what little they had.

Elise tried to take the spatula from him. "Let me do

that. I'm fine. You just startled me, that's all."

"Are you sure?"

"I'm positive," she said. "Now, tell me what you suspect happened to him."

Alex took a deep breath, and then he said, "Someone hit Mr. Brown over the head with one of the cast iron lighthouses that are in every cottage. I'm afraid that there's no doubt about it; it had to be murder."

Elise faltered again for just a moment before she managed to control herself. "Did you call the police?"

"I tried, but the cell phone towers must be out of commission from the storm. I can't get any reception, and neither could Jackson Benning. In case you're wondering, the landline doesn't work, either."

"Let me try my phone," she said as she handed him the spatula and left the room. Alex knew that Elise was shaken by the news of a guest's murder, but she was staying strong, something he knew that he could count on. When the rest of the world was falling down around him, Alex understood that Elise would be a rock for him, and he hoped that she could count on him as well.

She came back a minute later holding her cell phone. "I'm not getting anything, either. Oh well, it was worth a try. I let the Bennings go on and sit down in the dining room. You need to serve them. They're both pretty shaken up by what you found."

"They can wait a minute," Alex said as he pulled the pan of cooked eggs off the burner and wrapped Elise up in his arms. As he hugged her gently, he asked softly, "Is there anything I can do for you?"

"Just keep holding me," she answered, her voice muffled as she buried her head into his shoulder.

It always amazed him the way that Elise seemed to fit perfectly within his arms, as though the two of them together made one complete person. Alex held her close and gently stroked her hair, and as he did, he could feel the tension in her start to ease.

After a full minute, he asked softly, "Hey, are you okay?"

Elise pulled slightly away, looked up at him, gave him a quick kiss, and then she said, "I'm not yet, but I will be. Thanks. I needed that."

As she pulled completely away, Alex replied, "No more than I did."

"Poor Alex. Dead bodies seem to follow you around, don't they?"

"More than I'd like them to," he said. Alex glanced at the pan. "I've got a new rule. There will be no special orders today. It's scrambled eggs, biscuits, coffee, and juice. We still have coffee, don't we?"

"That's one thing we don't have to worry about. Our counterparts appear to be big fans of the stuff. And don't worry, there's juice in the fridge, too."

"How about lunch? Have you decided how you're going to handle that? Is there anything for dinner?" Since they were truly isolated now, he worried that they might run out of food before help arrived. He should have gone to the store when he'd had the chance, but he'd put the short-term needs of his guests above the long term, and now he was afraid they were all going to pay for it.

"We'll deal with that later," Elise said, a new cheerfulness in her voice that had been absent so recently. "Now go."

Alex nodded, knowing that there was nothing else he could do, so he grabbed the pot of coffee and a basket of hot biscuits and walked into the dining room. The Morrisons were in deep conversation with the Bennings, and they all looked expectantly at Alex when he joined them.

"What's going on, Alex?" Elizabeth asked. "These two have been spouting nonsense about you finding a dead body."

"Unfortunately, I'm afraid that it's true. Mr. Brown

has been murdered," he explained.

"I told you," Jackson Benning said, a glint of triumph in his eye.

Elizabeth chose to ignore him. "Are you absolutely sure that it was homicide?"

Alex wanted to say that if he was wrong, it was the oddest suicide he'd ever seen in his life, but this was no time for sarcasm. "Trust me, I'm sure."

"Have a lot of experience with dead bodies, do you?" Greg Morrison asked with a frown.

"More than I'd like to admit," Alex said. "I'm afraid wishing this away isn't going to do any of us any good. We're just going to have to pull together and get through this somehow until the police arrive."

"And when might that be?" Elizabeth asked him pointedly.

"I have no way of knowing, but my hunch is that it's going to be a while."

That certainly put an added chill in the air.

Chapter 8

To his surprise, it didn't take long for one of his guests to try to deny their situation.

"Well, you all can do as you please, but I'm not staying here another minute," Elizabeth declared after a moment's contemplation. "Come on, boys, we're leaving," she said as she stood and turned to her brothers.

"I'm afraid that's not possible," Alex said gravely.

"Do you think you can stop us?" Elizabeth asked pointedly. "You're most welcome to try, but I have to warn you, you will fail, and fail miserably."

"It's not me," Alex told her, ignoring the threat for the moment. It had been a challenge, but there was no reason to rise to the bait. "The drive is gone, and I'm wagering that the main road isn't any better."

"I told you that before, Elizabeth," John said. "I walked out and had a look at the drive up to the inn myself. Nobody's going anywhere until somebody comes by and digs us out."

Elizabeth dismissed her brother with one withering glance, and then she turned back to Alex. "I don't like this, sir. I don't like it one little bit."

"Don't think for one second that I do," Alex answered. "For now, we're just going to have to make the best of things until help arrives. Can I get you all coffee? We have biscuits, and eggs are soon to follow."

"We'll take three coffees," Greg said. "And some of those biscuits in your hand would be nice, too."

"Make that five," Jackson Benning added.

"Can do," Alex said as he filled up their cups. "Here you go. Scrambled eggs are coming up in a minute, and there's juice if anyone wants it. I'll be right back with the eggs and more biscuits."

Alex returned to the kitchen, grabbed another basket of biscuits as promised, and had to fight the temptation to have one himself. The innkeeper in him wouldn't allow it though. His guests came first, always.

After Alex made another trip to deliver the eggs, refreshed the biscuits, and then refilled their coffee cups, he returned to the kitchen to find Elise frowning.

The moment she saw him, she asked, "Alex, have you seen Dutch this morning?"

"No, I just figured he was sleeping in since he was sick."

Elise grabbed his arm. "I can't stop thinking about something. What if there was more than one victim last night?"

That thought had never even occurred to him. "I'll go check on him right now."

"Should you get one of the men to go with you?" Elise asked.

"No, I don't want to get them any more agitated than they already are. Don't worry about me. I'll be fine."

"Come back to me," she said as she kissed him hard and long. "Don't take any chances."

"I'll be careful. I promise," Alex said, and then walked out the back door so he wouldn't have to go back into the dining room and explain where he was headed.

His hand shook a little as he knocked on Dutch's door, and when there was no immediate reply, he felt a little queasiness in the pit of his stomach. After another knock, he tried the door handle.

It was locked.

Taking his master key out again, Alex unlocked door.

Dutch was on the bed, much as he'd found Mr. Brown earlier.

But thankfully, from the snores that were coming from the man, the caretaker was alive and well.

"What did you find?" Elise asked as he neared the kitchen. She had been standing outside on the small landing waiting on him. "I should have gone with you."

"Don't worry, he's fine."

"Are you sure about that?"

"He was snoring away when I left him," Alex said.

"Did you wake him and tell him what happened?"

Alex shook his head. "I didn't see any reason to do that. What can he do at this point? There's a dead body in one of the cottages, the road's out, and we don't have phone service or power. Why add to his worries along with him being sick?"

Elise glanced worriedly up at the sky. The dark clouds had won their earlier battle, and the sun was now gone again, apparently for good. The flatness of the land and the stark contrast of the dunes all made the place look as though it was on another world. "I don't like this, Alex. It looks like another storm is coming."

"If it does, there's nothing we can do about it. There's a murderer here with us, and we're all trapped together in the same snare." He hugged her again, and then he added, "Don't worry, we'll be all right."

"Just promise me that you won't leave me," Elise answered.

"Never," Alex replied, trying his best to put on a brave smile for her.

They walked back inside together, and Elise pulled two plates out of the oven. "Why don't you take a minute and eat? You must be starving."

"You didn't have to wait for me," Alex protested as she set them down on the counter.

"I didn't mind," she said. "Shall we eat here, or should we join our guests?"

"The truth is that I'd rather have you all to myself, but it might be better if we eat out there. I have a feeling they're all getting restless."

"Agreed," Elise said as she grabbed the plates.

There were more questions when they walked into the dining room, but Alex and Elise managed to eat in spite of them. What it all boiled down to was that there was no way to get away from the lighthouse inn. They would just have to wait until they were rescued by the outside world.

Alex just hoped that happened before the killer could strike again.

"We need to get out of here!" Jackson Benning told Alex emphatically as soon as the innkeeper finished his breakfast.

"I'm sorry, but you had to see the same thing that I did; the road's closed. There's no other way out."

"You don't understand. We *can't* stay." The man was standing so close to Alex he could feel his breath on his cheek.

"What can I do?" Alex asked. "The only way anyone's leaving here is on foot. I suppose you could walk around the dunes, or you could even take your chances walking along the beach, but there's no guarantee that there aren't washouts there as well. You could be going from having a safe, dry place to wait things out to putting you and Michelle in real jeopardy."

"You're just exaggerating because you don't want to lose our business," Jackson said. "We'll take the beach and make our way into town. I can't imagine there will be anything we can't walk around."

"Let's say there's nothing grave enough to make you turn back. Don't forget, it's seven miles, all on foot," Alex replied, "and there's no guarantee that things will be better even if you make it into town. All that being said, don't forget that the police are going to want to talk to you as soon as they hear about the murder out here. Do you think running away from the scene of the crime is going to look good to them?"

Jackson looked as though he wanted to hit Alex. "Why would they want to speak with us? We didn't do anything. We didn't even meet the man! We were in town eating dinner last night, and then we came back and headed straight back to our cottage after we talked to you."

"Then don't you think you should stay and explain it just like that to the police?" He could understand them not wanting to stay, but there were so many reasons to wait it out, it would be foolhardy to try getting away at this point.

Alex hadn't seen Michelle approach, and he didn't even realize she was there until she spoke. "He's right, Jackson. Everything Alex just said makes perfect sense. We can't leave."

"And I'm telling you, we're not staying, Michelle," he repeated, as if his comments were on some odd kind of loop. From the tone of his voice, it was clear he expected her to back down and accede to his wishes.

He was wrong. "I wish things were different," she answered softly, "but we don't have any choice. We're staying put until this mess is all sorted out."

Alex was surprised when the woman's husband acquiesced. It appeared to be the first argument Michelle had won in a very long time, based on her satisfied expression.

"Don't worry. I'm sure it won't take all that long," Alex said. "They're bound to dig us out of here soon." At least that was his fervent hope. He didn't want to be trapped at the inn with a murderer any more than anyone else did. If he had his druthers, he and Elise would be heading back to Hatteras West as fast as his old truck would take them, but that just wasn't an option, even if the roads had all been cleared. He'd made a promise to Harry and Barbara that he would treat their lighthouse inn as though it were his own, and there was nothing, short of dire circumstances, that could ever make him break that pledge.

Jackson didn't look as though he believed that help would arrive anytime soon. "And in the meantime, what are we supposed to do? There's a killer loose here, Alex. You realize that, don't you?"

"Trust me, I know better than anyone else," Alex said. "I have some advice, but I'm afraid it's pretty generic."

"I'm willing to listen to just about anything right now," Jackson said.

"Just be careful, stay around as many people as you can as much as you can manage it, and above all else, watch your back."

"That's good advice, but we're at the edge of nowhere in the cottage you put us in," he replied petulantly.

Per your request, Alex wanted to add, but he didn't. After all, he couldn't even blame the man for being snippy with him, given the circumstances. "We can take care of that. Why don't you move into the main quarters? You two can have my room, and I'll sleep on the couch. It's not much, but it's the best that I can do." It was going to be a hardship for Alex, but really, what choice did he have? He owed it to his guests to make them feel as safe as he could.

"We couldn't ask you to do that," Michelle said.

"Oh yes we could," Jackson interrupted. He'd given in once today, and Alex doubted that he'd be willing to bend again.

It was clear by Michelle's expression that she realized it as well.

"Thank you for your kindness," she said. "We'd be happy to take you up on your kind offer."

"Give me half an hour to clean your room, and then you can move in," Alex replied.

Michelle nodded as Jackson started to head back to

their cottage to pack their things. Before he left, he turned and said, "Alex, if you don't hear from us in ten minutes, come looking."

"Jackson, it will take us longer than that to pack," Michelle said.

"Not the way I'm planning to do it," he answered.

Alex hurried back inside and found Elise waiting for him. "What's going on? Did I hear you arguing with someone?"

"It was more of a discussion, really. I'm giving my room to the Bennings," he said. "They don't feel safe out there on the edge of the property in the last cottage, so I've volunteered to sleep on the couch and give them my bed."

"That's a good idea. I'll give my room to the Morrisons," she said. "I know there are three of them, and it's a tiny space, but they'll be able to manage, at least for a few nights."

"You don't have to do that."

"It's exactly what you're doing," Elise said. "So why shouldn't I? We're a team, remember?" He recognized that stubborn look on her face. Alex had known her long enough to realize it would be foolish to argue with her. She'd made up her mind, and that was the end of the discussion.

"Okay," he said, caving in. "You take the couch, and I'll sleep on one of the cots. We have several of those on hand, so if the Morrisons want to share your room, two of them will have to be on them."

"Care to guess who gets the bed?" Elise asked with a smile.

"If it's not Elizabeth, I don't have a clue," Alex said with a smile. It was nice to find even a kernel of amusement, given their current circumstances.

"Do you need help packing your things and cleaning your room?" she asked.

"If I'm going to be out of it in ten minutes, I do. Do

you mind lending me a hand?"

"No, after we do your room, we'll tackle mine," Elise answered.

Alex asked, "What if the Morrisons want to stay where they are?"

His question was soon answered as Elizabeth Morrison herself stormed into the building. "Mr. Winston, my brothers and I demand a room inside this main building. I've spoken with that other couple, the Bennings, and they tell me that you're giving them your lodging. I hate to be stuffy about it, but we expect the same courtesy."

"Are you saying that you don't mind sharing a room with both of your brothers?" Alex asked. "I'd hate to ask you to endure that kind of hardship on our account."

"There's no need to worry about us. We can manage just fine," she said. "We did it as children at our summer place, so there's no reason to believe that we can't manage it now."

"Give us twenty minutes then, and it's yours," Elise said.

It was clear Elizabeth had been expecting them to put up more of a fight. She clearly wasn't sure what to do with herself, a condition Alex doubted she'd experienced much in her life. "Why don't you go pack in the meantime, and tell your brothers to do the same? We'll have two cots set up in the room and have it cleaned as soon as we can."

"We won't wait over an hour," she said defiantly, doing her best to get a rise out of the innkeepers.

"It should be half that, if we can get busy right now," Elise said sweetly.

Elizabeth got the hint. "I'll leave you to it, then."

Working together, Alex and Elise soon had both rooms cleaned and their belongings packed away. It always amazed him how the most mundane tasks were more enjoyable when Elise was by his side. "We can store our bags in the hall closet for now," Alex said.

"I'm amazed we were able to fit two cots in that tiny little room. They're going to be bumping into each other all day in there."

"Thankfully, that's their problem, not ours," Alex said. "You're not going to make a fuss about taking the couch and leaving me a cot, are you?"

"Neither one looks all that comfortable to me, so I'm not sure who gets the better part of the deal. We'll flip for it later, how does that sound?"

"Fine by me. It appears that we're going to have our very own slumber party."

Elise nodded. "This isn't my idea of even a working vacation, but we'll manage. Alex, are you worried about a killer being amongst us? What if they strike again?"

He frowned. "I'm hoping that whoever killed the mysterious Mr. Brown had their own reasons to do it. If we're lucky, the killing spree is over."

"But what if it's not? What if he's just the first one to fall to the murderer?" Elise asked, the fear clear in her voice.

"I don't like it, but what can we do about it? I'll tell you what I told the Bennings. Walking that beach could be treacherous, and if we all stay together, there's a good chance that nothing else will happen." He had a sudden thought. "What about Dutch? Where are we going to put him? He can't just stay in that cottage of his, isolated from the rest of us."

She shrugged. "Like it or not, I guess he just volunteered to be our chaperone tonight."

Alex laughed wryly. "I'll go tell him the good news. It's time he woke up, anyway."

"What if he's still sick?"

"Elise, to be honest with you, I don't think there's much of anything wrong with him. Once he finds out what happened to our guest, my hunch is that he won't be able to wait to join us."

Alex started for the door and was surprised to find Elise on his heels. He turned and said, "You don't have to come with me, you know."

"I don't have to. I want to. From now on, we're on the buddy system, so hi, buddy."

"Hi," he said, and then he gave her a quick kiss. They might be pushed for time, but if ever there was a good reason to pause for a moment, that was surely it. "If I have to have a buddy, I'm just glad it's you."

She squeezed his hand. "Me, too. Right back at you."

They walked outside toward Dutch's cottage together, and Elise looked around. "This is the first time I've been out here today. That must have been some storm."

"According to our handyman, it's not all that unusual to have them this time of year. Funny, but Harry seems to have forgotten to mention it."

"Maybe, but I have a question for you. Did you tell him about the black bears that were spotted near Hatteras West last month?"

Alex smiled a little. "Now that I think about it, it may have slipped my mind, but that's not the same. The drought in the mountains brought them down out of the hills. Storms like this evidently happen much more frequently than that."

"You still didn't mention it, though. The truth of the matter is that I don't think either one of you wanted to jinx this lighthouse swap."

"You're probably right."

They got to Dutch's cottage, and after Alex knocked on the door three times, there was still no response.

Elise looked worried, but he tried to reassure her. "Don't worry, he didn't wake up before, either. I had to use my master key to check on him."

"Open the door, Alex. I've got a bad feeling about

this."

Alex did as Elise asked, and a tight knot formed in his gut as he opened the door. He wasn't at all sure what he would find there, but he had a hunch he wouldn't like it.

It was a relief finding the bed empty. Maybe Dutch was just getting out of the shower. Alex approached the small bathroom, but he found that it was empty as well.

Apparently their handyman had felt good enough to leave his cottage.

The question remained though, where had he gone?

Chapter 9

An hour later, much to Alex's relief and delight, the handyman walked into the main quarters, his pants and shoes thoroughly covered in wet sand. The entire roster of their guests were now in the lobby, trying to pretend that they didn't suspect each other of committing the murder that had driven them all together.

"Where have you been?" Alex asked. "We were worried about you."

"There was no need to be," Dutch said as he ran a hand through his long hair. "I wanted to see if we could walk out of here along the beach. I've got a feeling no one relishes the thought of staying here tonight without any power or running water, and that includes me."

"Can we make it out?" Jackson asked.

"Not a chance in the world," Dutch said. "The dunes are washed out about a mile from here toward town, and there's no way around them, unless you're prepared for a very rough swim. The waves are as big as I've seen them in ten years."

"What about in the other direction?" Elizabeth Morrison asked.

Dutch shook his head. "You could walk it, but there's nothing there until you hit the big bridge, and that's a dozen miles away, assuming there aren't any more washouts along the way. No, I'm afraid we're stuck here until the plows come and open the road back up."

"When might that be?" Elizabeth asked.

"It *might* be today," he said, and Alex saw several smiles, but then Dutch added, "But I sincerely doubt it. The truth is, we'll be lucky if they get to us by tomorrow."

"And if we're not lucky?" John Morrison asked.

"Three days, max. In the meantime, I suggest you folks do your best to enjoy your stay."

"That's kind of hard to do, what with the dead body and all," Jackson Benning said.

"Body? *What* body?" It was pretty clear this was news to Dutch, and Alex realized that he hadn't heard about the homicide yet.

"One of our guests died sometime last night," Alex said simply.

Elizabeth coughed. "That's hardly the proper way of describing it, Alex. You make it sound like it was from natural causes."

"Do you mean to tell me that it wasn't?" Dutch asked, clearly still having trouble wrapping his head around the concept.

"Someone used one of the small cast iron lighthouses on him," Elizabeth said in smug satisfaction. "Or so I've heard. I haven't seen the body myself. No one but Alex has."

"Are you sure he's dead?" Dutch asked.

"No doubt about it," Alex volunteered. "He was cold to the touch by the time I got to him."

Alex expected that to be accepted, but he was in for a rude surprise.

"So you continue to say. I want to see him for myself," Elizabeth said.

"I'm afraid that's not possible," Alex replied.

"Why shouldn't we be able to see him, too? My sister has a point," John answered.

"We *all* have a right to see him," Jackson added.

Alex was about to have a riot on his hands if he didn't do something, and fast. "People, I'm sure the police wouldn't appreciate us messing up their crime scene."

"Maybe not, but then again, they're not here, are they?" Dutch said.

"You're actually with them on this, Dutch?" Alex

asked.

"If it's murder, we all have a right to see it for ourselves," the handyman said stubbornly.

"It might be my right, but if it's all the same to you all, I believe that I'll pass on the opportunity," Michelle said. "I caught a glimpse of him when Alex and I found him. That was more than enough for me."

"Maybe, but it's not enough for me," her husband replied. "Come on, Alex. Either you let us in with the key, or we'll break the door down. You don't have a right to keep this from us."

Alex was about to protest further when Elise touched his arm lightly. "Alex, can I speak with you for a second?"

It was a reprieve, at least for the moment. "Hang on a second. Don't anybody do anything crazy while I'm gone. I'll be right back," he told them as he and Elise walked out onto the porch.

"Alex, you need to let them see for themselves, or I'm afraid that they really are going to break that door down. Did you hear the panic in their voices?"

"Elise, you know as well as I do that we could contaminate the crime scene if I open that door, and a killer could go free because of what I did. I'm not sure I can have that on my conscience." Alex couldn't stand the thought that something he did might allow someone to escape their just punishment. It was something that often haunted him during his amateur investigations.

"Alex, that's one thing I love about you, but you sensed the mood in there just as much as I did a minute ago. If you don't let them in, things could get ugly, and fast. At least this way you get to control the situation. Isn't that better than nothing?"

"I suppose you're right," Alex said. He could see Elise's point, but he still thought it was a bad idea. He was about to tell her that when the entire contingency of their guests came outside en masse.

"What's it going to be, Alex? Are you letting us in, or are we going to force our way in ourselves?" Jackson asked.

"There's no need for that. I'll unlock the door," Alex agreed.

"That's more like it," Elizabeth said.

Jackson started to walk with them when he noticed that Michelle wasn't coming. "Let's go. I'm not leaving you here by yourself."

"She can stay with me," Elise answered. "I've got to throw some sandwiches together for lunch, and I could use an extra set of hands."

"I'm afraid I won't be much help to you, Elise," Michelle said. "I was never really very good in the kitchen."

"Then I'll be glad for the company. You can sit on a stool and we can have a nice long chat while I work. How does that sound to you?"

She nodded, and then she glanced at her husband, who just shrugged in response. "Suit yourself, Michelle. Let's go, Winston. Make it happen."

Alex reluctantly stepped out in front of the crowd and made his way to the late Mr. Brown's cottage. It was pretty clear that Elise had been right. If he didn't give in, they'd do what they wanted to anyway.

Alex felt his hands tremble a little as he started to put the master key into the lock of the cottage door. Before he turned it, though, he looked back at his guests. "Let's get one thing straight. No one touches anything. Is that understood?"

"Just open the door," Jackson said. It was clear that he would make no such promise.

Well, at least he'd tried. Alex knew that he was fighting a losing battle. He unlocked the door and pulled it open. For a fleeting moment, he was afraid that the body was gone, but it was exactly as he'd left it

that morning, an event that seemed like it had happened
years before, not just a matter of hours.

Greg Morrison, upon seeing the body, immediately
pivoted away and ran toward the beach. He made it a
dozen steps before he fell to his knees and began to
throw up in the sand.

Elizabeth looked at her brother with distaste. "He
always was the weakest link among us." She turned
back to the body, and then she complained, "Mr.
Winston, we can't see his face from the way he's lying.
Turn him over."

"*What?*" Alex asked incredulously. "You've got to
be kidding me."

"Now that I think about it, I realize that I haven't
seen his face since we first arrived," Elizabeth
explained. "He managed to hide it last night even as he
was fleeing the dining room. John, did you get a clear
look at him?"

"No," her brother admitted.

She turned to Jackson Benning. "And you?"

"No, I never saw him. Then again, Michelle and I
went out to dinner, and then straight back to our cottage
because of the rain."

"Then we must all get a look at him," Elizabeth said.
"Alex, if you're squeamish, I'll do it myself. I was a
mortician's assistant for two years in college. I'm not
afraid to handle a dead body."

He wasn't sure what to make of that. "I still say that
we shouldn't touch him. I think it's a very bad idea."

"Nonsense," Elizabeth said as she stepped past Alex
before he could react.

"Don't do it," Alex commanded, an order that was
quickly ignored.

Elizabeth Morrison flipped Mr. Brown over, and
then they all looked down at the body. Alex wasn't
certain what reaction he was expecting, but the slight
nod she gave wasn't even on the list. "There, that

wasn't so bad, was it?"

"Did you know him?" he asked her.

Elizabeth frowned, and then after a moment, she shook her head. "No, I'm afraid not."

Alex was about to ask the other three men standing there when he spotted the gray sheen on Jackson Benning's face.

"Jackson, you recognize him, don't you? Don't bother trying to deny it. It's written all over your face."

Jackson nodded once, and then he explained, "That's the man who's been following us."

Chapter 10

"Following you? What are you talking about?"
Alex asked.

"That man's been tailing us for the past three days.
The first few times I saw him, I thought it was just a
coincidence, but now there's no doubt in my mind. It's
just too hard to swallow that his presence here is
random. What could he possibly want with us?"

"Maybe we should ask Michelle that same
question," Alex suggested. There was clearly
something going on here, but what could it be?

Jackson shook his head as he frowned. "There's no
way I'm going to make her come in here and look that
dead body in the face."

"That's not a problem. I'll take a picture of him
with my phone," John Morrison said as he did exactly
that. After taking a quick picture, he said, "At least it's
good for something, even if I can't call out on it. We
can show her the photo, and that way she doesn't have
to see the body itself again."

"But that still doesn't answer who he is, or was,
actually," Elizabeth said. "We should search his
pockets to see if we can find anything there."

"There's no way I'm going to allow anyone to do
that. That's way over the line," Alex said, feeling the
situation slipping faster and faster through his fingers
like dry sand. He, too, was curious about the late Mr.
Brown, and if he'd been back in Elkton Falls, he would
have most likely suggested the search himself, but he
was a stranger in a strange land here, and he had no idea
how the police would react when they learned that
amateurs, no matter how well intentioned, were
searching dead bodies.

"I don't think it's inappropriate at all," Elizabeth

said as she patted the corpse down efficiently. She truly wasn't afraid of touching Brown's dead body at all. In a million years, Alex never would have guessed that Elizabeth Morrison had it in her. No wonder her brothers were more than a little bit afraid of the woman. Alex had to wonder if that wasn't the prudent way to feel, after seeing her clinical approach to what would send most people screaming in the other direction. "Odd. There's nothing here."

She left the body, headed directly to the dresser, and then quickly began opening the drawers. The only thing she found was a single car key, and the cottage's key on its lighthouse chain.

"He has no wallet, no ID, and no cash on him that we can find. How did he pay you?" she asked Alex.

"Cash," Alex admitted.

"And you didn't ask him for identification?" Jackson asked.

That sounded too much like an accusation for Alex's taste. "Of course I did. I was about to turn him away, but he offered me a credit card to cover any damages."

"What was the name on the card?" Jackson asked.

"Marsh Enterprises," Alex said. "Does that mean anything to anybody?"

No one had a clue.

"Maybe there's something in his car," John suggested.

"Let's go see," Elizabeth said, clearly done with the body and the premises. As she stepped away, Alex noticed that she slipped something into her pocket.

"What was that?" he asked.

"What are you talking about? You're delusional, Alex."

"I saw you just slip something into your pocket," Alex insisted. "I demand to know what you found."

"I didn't find anything!" she protested. "I don't appreciate you calling me a thief!"

John bristled. "Mr. Winston, my sister is many things, but she doesn't steal, especially not from the dead."

Alex wasn't about to back down, though. "I don't care how long and how hard you defend her. I saw what I saw."

"You're imagining things," Elizabeth said. She reached into both pockets and pulled the linings out, showing that there was nothing there.

"What more can I do? Do you want to strip-search me, or are you satisfied?" She stared hard at him, daring him to say another word.

Alex might have been impressed by her fierceness, but he wasn't about to back down. After all, he'd faced killers before. Was he facing one now? Had Elizabeth found something that implicated her or her brothers? That might explain why she'd been so willing to search the body. No matter what the consequences might be, he had to know. "How about your hands? You could have easily palmed whatever you took."

"This is getting utterly ridiculous," Elizabeth said. "You're just an innkeeper."

"Maybe so, but I know what I saw, and no amount of blustering and bullying on your part is going to convince me otherwise. I want to see your hands," he repeated, wondering if the next thing he was going to feel was a blow from behind.

Elizabeth appeared to consider pushing past him to get out the door, but finally, she sighed and opened her hands with a snarling expression on her face.

There was a pack of matches there.

"Are you satisfied? I promised my brothers I'd quit smoking, but stress brings the craving out in me. I have a single cigarette in my luggage but no way to light it. I saw the matches, and I took them."

"Elizabeth," John said accusingly. "You promised."

"What can I say? I had a moment of weakness.

Forgive me," she said.

Alex held out a hand. "I want to see that pack myself."

"You've really gotten paranoid all of a sudden, haven't you?" Elizabeth asked him.

Jackson, for a change of pace, was on Alex's side. "What's the harm in showing him, then, lady? I wouldn't mind seeing them myself."

Elizabeth handed the pack over to him, and Alex flipped the cover open. There wasn't anything obvious at first, and he was about to hand them back to her when he noticed that there was writing on the side covered by the matches. Only a handful of discarded matches revealed that anything had been written there at all.

Printed in all capitals, Alex read: "M w/ B. M 2?"

What on earth could that mean?

Alex read the letters aloud, and Elizabeth reached for the book of matches after he finished. Alex had a hunch that if he gave the pack to her, he'd never see it again. Instead, he carefully tore the cover with the writing off, leaving the striking strip and matches intact, but keeping the penned note for himself. "There you go. You wanted matches. You got matches."

The guest didn't look at all happy about his action, but there was really nothing she could do about it if what she'd said were true.

As they all walked out of the cottage, Alex asked, "Are you just going to leave him like that? At least flip him back over the way we found him."

Elizabeth shrugged, and then she reached down with one hand and turned the late Mr. Brown back in the position where Alex had first discovered him.

They were at the rental car when Elizabeth flipped the keys to her brother Greg, now recovered from his queasiness.

"Feeling any better?" she asked.

He merely nodded.

"Good. We need to check out Brown's car."

"What exactly are we looking for?" Greg asked.

"I don't really know, but a clue would be nice."

"To what, exactly?"

"His identity, why he was murdered, what he was doing here; take your pick," Jackson Benning said.

Greg nodded as he unlocked the car. Alex had lost complete control over the group, and all he could do now was stand close and see if they found anything else. He needed to take a more proactive role, since his earlier hesitation could have easily cost them all what might turn out to be a vital clue in the man's murder. Greg opened every door, so at least they could all watch as he went over the car from top to bottom.

"He's a fanatic about automobiles," Elizabeth explained. "If there's anything there, Greg will find it."

After a brief but thorough search, Greg stood and said, "There's nothing."

"Are you sure?" Jackson asked.

"I checked everything. Something was odd."

"What's that?" John asked.

"There wasn't even a contract in the glove compartment, though clearly it's a rental car. Somebody must have gotten to it before we did."

"Maybe the killer cleaned it out after he killed Brown," Jackson said.

"Why would anyone want to steal a rental agreement?" Alex asked, though he had a sneaking suspicion that he knew exactly why someone might do it.

"We don't know who Brown really is, do we? I'd say that if that was the murderer's goal, they succeeded, wouldn't you?" Elizabeth asked.

"But how did they know we wouldn't be able to just call the police for help? There have to be records kept with the car company. It can't be that hard to find out if you know how to work the official channels," Greg said.

Alex decided it was time to share his theory with the group. It might be dangerous, in a way warning the killer that he was no mere innkeeper, but really, what choice did he have? "Maybe he didn't kill Mr. Brown until after the storm, when he knew he'd be safe for the moment."

"Or she," Jackson added as he glanced at Elizabeth.

"Are you accusing me of something?" she asked harshly, turning on him.

"I'm just saying, we're all suspects here," Jackson answered with a shrug.

"Including your wife," Elizabeth said.

"And your brothers as well," he countered.

"Don't forget the inn staff," Elizabeth said. "Any one of them could just as easily have done it. Alex and Elise claim they aren't from around here, but how do we really know that?" She looked hard at Dutch as she added, "It was awfully convenient for you to be sick last night, wasn't it?"

"I'm no killer, lady," Dutch protested.

She merely shrugged at his denial. "The truth is, anybody stranded here could be the killer. In fact, we can safely say that one of us did it."

The real question was, which one? Alex had heard enough accusations without justification. It wasn't the first time he'd ever been named as a murder suspect, but that still didn't mean he had to like it. "We're not getting anywhere debating who *might* be guilty. Let's lock the car up, take the keys into the main building, and see if Michelle has ever seen the man before."

"I told you before, he was following us," Jackson said. "I'm willing to bet that she'll recognize him, too."

"I'd like to hear her say that as well," Elizabeth replied. "We all would." She paused in front of the man and added, "If you give her the slightest clue, the least hint, we're going to lock you up in chains until the police get here. Do you understand?"

"Have you lost your mind, woman?" Jackson asked incredulously.

"No, but if any of us notice the slightest indication that you're cueing your wife, you'll be sorry."

"Fine, show her the picture," Jackson said, clearly disgusted with the idea. "I won't say a word."

"As a matter of fact, you should stay out of the room entirely," Elizabeth said. "Greg. Stay with him. If he tries to come in, stop him."

Alex wasn't sure that was really necessary, but he could understand the precaution, so he kept his misgivings to himself, at least for the moment.

They all walked into the kitchen, and Elizabeth said to Michelle, "We hate to ask, but you need to do this, no matter how unpleasant it is."

"Do what?" she asked, clearly disturbed by his words. "Where's Jackson? What happened to him?"

"He's fine," Elizabeth said smoothly. "Right now he's helping Greg with something, but he'll be right in."

John showed Michelle the picture on his phone and asked her, "Think carefully. Have you ever seen this man before?"

Michelle glanced at the image and then looked quickly away.

"No," she said.

Elizabeth's voice was more urgent now. "Look again, Michelle. This is important."

"I don't want to," she said plaintively.

"Leave her alone," Elise protested.

Alex touched her arm as he softly said, "Elise, this is necessary. I'm sorry, but we wouldn't ask if it weren't important."

She seemed to take that in, and then she said, "I'll look first, then."

Greg pointed the phone toward her.

Elise nodded and then said, "That's the man who

checked in as Mr. Brown yesterday."

Michelle looked at the image again, and then a puzzled look crossed her face. "I was wrong just now. I *have* seen him before."

"Here at the inn?" Alex asked, despite the dirty look Elizabeth shot in his direction.

"No, he's the man who's been following us. Wait for Jackson. He'll tell you."

"Go get him," Elizabeth told John, who left to get the two men.

"What's going on?" Michelle asked.

Jackson stormed into the room and pushed the phone away. "I told them, but they wouldn't believe me. I'm sorry to put you through that."

Michelle asked, "What's going on? Who was he? Why was he here? Do you have any idea why he was following us?"

"We're not sure about any of that," Jackson said.

Elizabeth explained, "There was no identification on him. Anywhere."

"That's crazy," Elise said. "He paid us yesterday."

"That was in cash," Alex reminded her. "There was no sign of his credit card, either."

"Well then, someone else must have taken them. Don't you remember? He took the money from his wallet when he paid for his room. I saw him do it."

Alex frowned. "I didn't see it."

"That's because you were getting his registration form ready," she said. "I know what I saw. His wallet was brown leather, and it looked really old."

"Then where is it now?" Jackson asked her.

"How should I know? All I know is that he had it on him yesterday."

Dutch said, "Hang on a second." He dug into his pants pocket and pulled out an old wallet. "Is this the wallet you're talking about?"

Elise nodded. "Where did you get that?"

"Did you take it off the body after you killed him?" Elizabeth asked him pointedly.

Dutch shook his head in disbelief. It was clear that some of the people gathered in the kitchen didn't believe Dutch's story, especially given the way he looked. He'd never be mistaken for a banker or a lawyer, or in fact, anyone currently holding a job. The man looked like a drifter, though he'd come highly recommended by Harry and Barbara. Until Alex knew otherwise, he wasn't going to condemn him. "It was in the surf. I found it when I was looking for a way out of here this morning. It was washed up on the beach, so I picked it up."

Alex asked, "May I see it?"

Dutch nodded. "Sure. I've got nothing to hide, but that's the way I found it. There was nothing inside it at all."

Alex took the wallet and felt the dampness in it. One whiff was enough to tell him that it had been in the ocean, at least for a brief time. That helped Dutch's story, unless he'd been the one to dunk it into the waves himself. Alex hated being suspicious of everyone, but he really had no choice. There was a murderer amongst them, and he couldn't drop his guard, not even for a second.

The first thing Alex did was open the wallet to look for any money.

It was empty.

Chapter 11

Jackson asked, "Are you sure there wasn't any cash or credit cards in it when you found it, Dutch?"

"What are you accusing me of, mister? I know some people might judge me by the way I look, but I'm not a thief."

"Take it easy," Alex said. "We're just trying to get as much information as we can."

Dutch frowned. "Like I said before, it was empty when I found it."

"Where exactly was that?" Alex asked, having a sudden inspiration.

"Not far from here," Dutch said.

"Show me."

"We're coming, too," the Morrisons said, as well as Jackson Benning.

"We'll stay back here, if you don't mind," Elise said. "Lunch will be ready soon."

"This shouldn't take long," Alex promised.

The body of investigators walked to the beach, and Dutch pointed to where he'd found the wallet. They all spread out, and it didn't take long for Greg to find something.

It was a plastic sleeve that had been in the wallet before someone had thrown it into the ocean. Clearly they'd been trying to destroy the evidence without any knowledge that waves had a tendency to wash things back up onto shore.

"What's in there?" Alex asked as he approached Greg.

"Let's see. There's a driver's license and a few business cards in there, but there's no money," he said as he pulled out the soaked paper cards and the plastic license.

Alex took the license and saw that it was from North Carolina, with a Charlotte address. Mr. Brown was clearly a long way from home, nearly as far as Alex and Elise were from their lighthouse.

"What's his real name?" Jackson asked, trying to see for himself.

"Steve Danvers," Alex replied as he read it off the license. "Does that name ring any bells to any of you?"

If it did, no one admitted it, but Greg might have flinched just a little when he heard it.

Alex took that in, and then he returned his attention to the rest of their findings. There were three business cards, identical, and worse for the wear after being dunked in the ocean.

The name on them matched the driver's license.

"It appears that the late Mr. Danvers, aka Mr. Brown, was a private detective," Alex said. "Let's go back inside."

Jackson didn't seem particularly shocked by the news. The Morrisons were all hard to read, but Alex had a feeling that Greg knew the name before he'd spoken it aloud.

Once they were all gathered back in the kitchen with Elise and Michelle, Alex didn't want to ask the next obvious question, but he really had no choice. "Could there be a reason Danvers has been following the two of you?" he asked Jackson and Michelle.

She might have said something, but Jackson spoke before she could. "There's no reason that we know of."

Elise asked softly, "Michelle, is that true?"

She wouldn't make eye contact with Elise; she just shook her head.

"What about the three of you?" he asked, looking at the Morrison clan now.

"Our lives are open books," Elizabeth said. "We had no reason to come into contact with a private investigator before we came here."

"Dutch?" Alex asked. "How about you?"

The handyman laughed. "Alex, my net worth is just over forty-seven dollars. It's in a shoebox under my bed, if you want to rob me. I've got nothing that's valuable to anyone else in the world." He paused, and then he looked hard at Alex and then Elise. "No offense, but how about you two? I don't know you any more than you know me, and I can't exactly call Harry and ask him about you. Have you two done anything that might merit the attention of a PI? You two aren't married, at least to each other. How about to someone else, though? Why would a private detective follow you two here from Charlotte?"

Alex was about to protest when he saw Michelle's face go pale. Apparently Dutch had hit a nerve, but not with them. He explained, "Elise and I aren't married, to each other or anyone else." He turned to Michelle. "Can you say the same thing?"

"I'm not really married to Malcolm anymore, at least not in my heart," she said, her words tumbling out of her. "Jackson and I are married in spirit, and that's all that counts."

"You just had to tell them, didn't you?" Jackson shouted at her.

"Keep your voice down, sir," Elise commanded. "Michelle, are you at least separated from your husband?"

"Of course I am. We've been apart nearly a year. As a matter of fact, the divorce will be final in two days. I can't believe it takes a year in North Carolina before a divorce becomes official."

Alex thought about that, and then he asked, "I'm curious about something, so if you'd indulge me, this can go much faster. Michelle, is there any money involved in the divorce settlement?"

"How did you know?" Michelle asked him.

Elizabeth answered for him. "It's more than just a

lucky guess. I was wondering the same thing. How much are we talking about here?"

"That's *not* why we're together," Jackson insisted, raising his voice again. "We're in love."

"So then, you're saying that money's not a factor." Elizabeth looked as though she didn't believe it for an instant.

"Of course it isn't," he snapped.

"Is it over a hundred thousand dollars or under?" John asked.

Before Jackson could stop her, Michelle admitted, "Oh, it's a lot more than that."

John nodded. "And I'm willing to bet that if your husband could prove you were having an affair, you'd get a lot less in the settlement. Thus the private detective following you around."

"I've already been warned about that. That's why we've been so careful," Michelle complained. Alex liked the woman, and he even felt sympathy for her being trapped in a marriage she no longer wanted to be a part of, but the discovery gave him a huge reason to suspect that she or her cohort had committed murder to save themselves a great deal of money.

"Apparently not careful enough," Dutch said, chiming in when it really wasn't needed.

Elizabeth frowned. "It's simple, then. One of them did it. They didn't want to lose the money from the settlement, and when the PI showed up, they knew they had to do something to stop him from reporting back before the divorce became final."

Jackson snapped, "I don't like your tone or the implication of what you're saying, lady."

John moved in close to him. "Watch how you speak to my sister."

Jackson backed up a step. "She's the one who'd better be careful. I don't like being accused of murder."

"But you're fine with adultery," Elizabeth said.

"A year is insane," Jackson snapped. "It's way too long to wait for true love."

"Some might argue that's not true, but while that might be up for debate, the money is a tangible fact pertaining to the case," Elizabeth said.

"I'm done talking about it," Jackson said. "Come on, Michelle. We're getting out of here, no matter what it takes."

"We've already discussed it. There's no way out, Jackson," Michelle said. "You heard what Dutch said."

"He could be lying, or he could be wrong. Either way, I'm not hanging around here. Are you coming with me or not?"

She was about to answer when Elise said, "Michelle, you don't have to go with him, you know. You can stay here with us."

"Can you keep me safe?" Michelle asked.

Elise couldn't meet her eyes, and Alex couldn't promise Michelle anything, either. He wasn't even certain that in the end, he'd be able to keep Elise and himself alive.

"That's what I thought," Michelle said. "Thanks anyway, but I'll take my chances with Jackson."

There was nothing Alex could do to stop them. After all, they weren't his captives, and he had no authority to make them stay. All he had was reason on his side.

"Think about how this will look to the police when they get here," Alex argued. "Do you really want that spotlight on you by running away?"

"We're not running anywhere," Jackson said. "We all know about the private investigator now, so staying here doesn't help us at all. The only way we'll be safe is by getting away from this inn."

Jackson flung open the back door, and Alex realized that the rain and wind had picked up again while they'd been inside talking.

It appeared that they were in for another round of storms.

He wouldn't want to take the hike that Jackson and Michelle were about to, but then again, it wasn't his decision.

"Good luck, then," he said.

Elise pled with him, "Alex, you have to stop them."

"I can't, not unless we lock them up in one of the cottages."

Elizabeth said, "That's not a bad idea. We can't just let a killer go free. They might never be found again."

Alex looked steadily at her. "The truth is, we still can't be sure one of them is the murderer."

She looked surprised by the comment. "What possible motive would any of us have to kill that man? He wasn't following any of us."

"There are more motives for murder than that," Alex said.

"Such as?" John asked.

"There are a great many reasons people kill, from protecting someone they love or keeping a secret, wanting revenge, to wanting something someone else has. The list goes on and on."

"We don't have *any* of those motives," Elizabeth said, "and I won't allow you to accuse us of things we didn't do. Come on, guys, let's go to our room."

After they were gone, Dutch asked, "Is there any chance I could get a bite to eat? I'm feeling a lot better, and I'm really starving."

Alex was going to tell him no, that he'd lost his opportunity to eat, but Elise was too kindhearted for that. "We're having sandwiches for lunch, but I could heat up a couple of biscuits and some coffee for you in the meantime, if you'd like. It won't take a minute."

"Thanks, I'd appreciate that."

As Elise put the pan of leftover biscuits back in the oven to reheat, Dutch said, "Listen, I didn't mean anything by what I said before. I don't think either one of you killed anybody."

"Thanks," Alex said.

It was clear that Dutch was waiting for something else. When Alex didn't respond in kind, Dutch asked, "Does that mean that you still think I might have done it myself?"

Alex just shrugged. "As far as I'm concerned, everyone but Elise and I are suspects. We all had the opportunity, and the means was right there in his room. All that's left is figuring out the motive."

"But that's the tricky part, isn't it? I've read enough mysteries to know that not many folks kill for no reason at all."

"There might be something there for everyone as well; we just don't know what it is yet."

"You don't trust anybody, do you?" Dutch asked him in wonder.

"I'd put my life in Elise's hands, and you met the only other two people I trust with everything I have; they just left yesterday. Mor is my best friend after Elise, Emma is his wife, and I'd stake my life on any one of them."

"It must be nice to have that," Dutch said with a sad shake of his head.

Alex realized that the handyman must not have had many friends of his own. He was about to say something when Elise presented the handyman with two warmed biscuits and jelly, along with a cup of coffee.

Dutch took it all gratefully from her and said, "If you don't mind, I'll have this out on the porch. I want to see what this storm's doing."

"You need to grab a few things from the cottage so you can come stay with us here," Alex said.

Dutch shook his head. "Thanks, but I'm fine right where I am."

"Dutch, it isn't safe being alone." Alex didn't want

to mention the fact that he'd sleep better if everyone was accounted for.

The handyman seemed to chew that over. "I'll think about it. Now, do you care if I go?"

"Don't be silly. We don't mind at all," Elise answered.

After they were alone, Elise moved quickly into his arms. "Would you mind holding me again, Alex?"

He didn't need to be asked twice. As he put his arms around her, Alex felt her shiver against him. She was shaken by the murder and what they'd learned since more than she'd shown. Only when they were alone did Elise trust herself to let it out. She cried for just a moment, but quickly stopped it. As she pulled away, Elise used her hand to wipe away her tears. "Sorry about that."

"Don't be," he said. "There's nothing wrong with being human."

"I just wish there was something we could do. Alex, I hate feeling so helpless."

"I do, too, but we're just going to have to ride this out." He looked out the window and saw the rain was picking up, coming down in sheets now. There was no way Jackson and Michelle were going to make it anywhere. He just hoped they found their way back to the inn.

Then again, maybe getting rid of two suspects in the storm wasn't a bad idea after all.

Chapter 12

Twenty minutes later, just before they were going to serve lunch, there was a pounding on the kitchen door.

Alex had been expecting it, so he wasn't even a little surprised when he held it open and Michelle and Jackson stumbled in, soaking wet. Elise grabbed a handful of towels from the closet and handed them to the soaked pair.

"Have any luck making it into town?" Alex asked them with a smile.

"We didn't get very far," Jackson admitted. "It's getting brutal out there. The wind is whipping the sand up, and it kept getting in our eyes."

"At least you left your bags here with us," Elise said. "Your spare clothes will be dry." They'd abandoned their luggage, so at least they had that going for them. "I'm afraid the water heater is electric, so the shower is going to be cold."

"At this point, we'll take whatever we can get," Michelle said, clearly on the point of bursting into tears. "I'm so sorry we ran off like that."

"No worries. It was understandable, given the day you've had," Elise said. "I'm glad you're back, and safe. That's really all that matters."

Michelle took another step into the kitchen, and then she realized that she was dripping all over the floor. "We'll come back after we're in fresh clothes and clean that up." She looked immediately at Jackson, who was obviously about to protest. "Right, Jackson?" she asked.

"Right," he answered grumpily.

After the pair walked through the dining room and into the lobby, Alex grabbed a mop. Elise smiled at him as he started working on the floor. "You have a good heart, you know that, don't you?"

"I just don't want to see the floors ruined," he answered with a shrug.

"Alex Winston, that heart pine will last longer than any of us will. Admit it. You're just a big softie deep down where it counts."

"Fine, believe whatever you want to believe," he said with a grin as he continued to mop the floor.

As he started to disappear out of the dining room, Elise asked, "Where are you going?"

"I don't really have much choice, do I? I'm going to follow their trail," Alex replied.

"Hang on a second. I'll go with you," she answered, and Alex nodded.

"That's what the buddy system is all about. Is lunch ready?"

"It will be as soon as we serve it. I'm afraid there is going to be some grumbling from our guests. In order to have a decent dinner tonight, lunch is going to be the bare minimum, and that means peanut butter and jelly sandwiches for everyone."

"I have a feeling you won't get any complaints from them today," Alex said.

"Wanna bet?" she asked.

"Not a chance," Alex answered with a smile.

By the time Alex finished mopping the floors and he and Elise got back into the dining room, they found the Morrisons already waiting on them.

"We're hungry," Greg said.

Elizabeth added, "But take your time. We're more than happy to wait."

She said the last bit to Greg, and though it was clear he wasn't all that happy about the prospect of waiting to eat, he clearly didn't want to cross his sister, either. "Yeah, there's no rush," he added.

"It'll just be a minute," Elise assured them as she

and Alex went into the kitchen.

There were a few puddles in there as well that he'd missed earlier, but it was too late to get them now. Alex had left the mop by the door of the bedroom where Michelle and Jackson were cleaning up. As an innkeeper, he frowned on folks who made a mess in his place of business, but this couldn't be helped, given the couple's determination to try to overcome the elements, a mission he was sure they would fail at. The messy floor was evidence enough of that. He didn't like it, but he'd just have to deal with it.

After the Morrisons were served their lunches, Dutch came in, grabbed a sandwich, but instead of hanging around, he left to eat it on the covered porch.

Alex looked at Elise and asked, "Are you ready to eat?"

"I am if you are."

The allotted lunch hour was nearly over when Michelle and Jackson finally joined them. They each took a plate and grabbed a sandwich apiece, along with cups of coffee, no doubt to warm them both up. There were potato chips as well, and cookies for dessert, though they were all store-bought. Alex knew that Elise prided herself on her cooking, but there wasn't much she could do with the supplies she had on hand. He was sure she'd somehow manage to feed them all until someone came along and rescued them.

In the meantime, they'd just make do. Alex's only goal now was to keep everyone alive.

He just wished he had a clue on how to go about it.

After lunch, everyone reconvened in the lobby of the main quarters, including Dutch. The rain was starting to really pick up again, and Alex regretted not being able to get more information about the storm. Surely there had to be some kind of weather-band radio somewhere, but Harry had failed to mention it, and Alex wished he could call his distant friend. It was amazing how isolated he felt without power and communication.

Elizabeth asked, "What are we all supposed to do now?"

Alex answered, "To be honest with you, I have no idea. There's not much more we can do but wait until someone starts to wonder about us."

"Come on. You're an innkeeper, even if you're not at your own inn. Surely you have *some* ideas," Elizabeth said.

Alex looked around the room and saw a shelf on the bookcase housing many popular board games. "It's a little wet outside for a nature walk," he said. As Elizabeth Morrison began to cloud up, Alex quickly added, "We could always pass the time playing games."

Jackson looked at the shelf. "Should we play Clue? If you're game, I've already got a guess. I think it was Elizabeth Morrison in the cottage with the cast iron lighthouse. I'm joking, of course," he added when he saw the dirty looks all three Morrisons were giving him.

"Not funny, Mr. Benning, not funny at all," Elizabeth said with a frown. "Anyone care for a game of chess?"

Both of her brothers shook their heads silently in unison, but if Jackson saw it, he chose to ignore it. "Sure, I'll be happy to thump you."

A gleam entered Elizabeth's eyes. "We'll just see about that."

Greg and John Morrison looked at each other wearily. "Checkers?" Greg asked.

"Why not?" John replied.

That left Alex, Elise, Dutch, and Michelle. "I suppose we could play bridge," Michelle said.

"Never learned the game," Dutch said. "Poker?"

"How about Hearts?" Elise suggested. "If you don't know how to play, it's an easy game to learn."

"I play," Dutch admitted.

Alex turned to Michelle. Jackson and Elizabeth were already setting up the chessboard. She smiled softly. "That would be a nice distraction from all of this."

They all played their games, and Alex paid more attention to his guests than he did the competitions. It seemed that Elizabeth Morrison was quite good at chess, but to everyone's surprise, Jackson Benning might have been just a shade better. From the way the chess pieces were being slammed down on the board, Alex was glad the set didn't belong to him. The brothers, on the other hand, seemed to enjoy the simpler strategy of checkers, and Alex wondered if they were secretly enjoying their sister's battle. As for Hearts, Dutch showed a surprising acuity for the game, making Alex realize something he should have known anyway. It was important not to judge people by the way they looked or dressed. After all, he had a friend back in Elkton Falls with more money than he could dream of who dressed like a field hand most days. So then, who was the murderer among these folks gathered here? It was clear that Michelle and Jackson had motives, and strong ones at that. Holding onto a windfall of money would be motive enough for a great many people, and he doubted these two were the exception. He liked Michelle, though he wasn't all that fond of Jackson. Still, that didn't make either one of them innocent or guilty. As to the Morrisons, Alex suspected they knew more than they were letting on. Greg had visibly flinched when he'd seen Brown's picture, and Elizabeth had been a little too calculating in his cottage, taking charge of the search herself and practically climbing over the body in search of clues. Then she'd hidden the one item they had found, though Alex still had no idea what it meant.

M w/ B. M 2?

What could it mean? Could the M stand for Michelle, or even Morrison? Why the 2? Was w/B

with Benning? Michelle was with Benning. That fit.
Then again, it could have meant Meet with Brown.
Could the PI have taken the name of another subject of
investigation when pressed for a name? It wouldn't
surprise him. Another thought occurred to him. What if
it meant Meet with Dutch? Dutch was a nickname, and
for all Alex knew, his real name could be Mortimer.
Could the inn's handyman be involved in this somehow,
despite all of his protestations? Dutch came and went as
he pleased, and Alex wondered if he had a master key to
the cottages himself. That would have allowed him to
creep into the private detective's room and kill him in
his sleep. But what motive could he have had?

And what about M2? There were three Morrisons,
so which two made the list?

Alex realized that he didn't have enough
information yet, but if they were going to be stuck there
together, he was determined to find out what had really
happened to the private investigator. If he could, he'd
love to be able to give the police the name of the
murderer if they ever showed up.

"Alex, it's your turn," Elise prompted him, bringing
him back from his thoughts. "You're really distracted
this afternoon, aren't you?"

The innkeeper looked outside at the pounding rain,
trying to come up with an excuse other than the truth
that he could give them all, but Dutch supplied it for
him. "It's the weather, isn't it?"

"It just came on all of a sudden," Alex agreed,
happy to be able to say something. "I'm surprised
Harry doesn't have a battery-operated weather radio on
the premises."

Dutch looked surprised by the statement. "He does.
It's under the desk, along with some batteries. I thought
you knew about it. He told me right before he left that
he was putting it on his list."

The lists Alex and Harry had exchanged covered

nearly every contingency either innkeeper could think of. They were volumes more than mere notes, and Alex had forgotten all about them. He stood and walked over to the desk. Sure enough, buried under a discarded Acadia sweatshirt was an all-weather radio, along with some batteries. He loaded the radio, and then he flipped it on. After a brief burst of static, they all heard a looped weather forecast from the National Weather Center.

"...storm and high tide warnings for the Outer Banks effective until six p.m. tomorrow. Heavy downpours at times, flooding a possibility throughout the broadcast area..."

They all stopped their games to listen through the loop twice. It appeared that there would be no rescue tomorrow, either.

Alex said as much, and Dutch corrected him, saying, "It sounds like a monster of a storm, so my guess is we'll be here at least two more days."

"Do we have enough food to last that long?" John Morrison asked.

Elise nodded. "It might not be fancy, but we won't go hungry."

"How about fresh water?" Elizabeth asked.

Dutch took that one. "We have town water, so as long as their generator is working, we'll be fine. It won't be hot, though. The heater's electric, as some of you have already found out." He looked at Jackson and Michelle as he mentioned the last point.

"But we had biscuits this morning, and the power was out then, too," Michelle said.

"Thankfully the oven and stovetop are both gas," Elise explained.

"So, we're in decent shape," Greg said.

Jackson looked at him as though he'd lost his mind. "You mean besides the fact that one of us is a killer? Oh, yes, we're all just dandy."

"You know what I meant," Greg said.

"We all do," Elizabeth answered, coming to her brother's defense. She glanced down at the chessboard and tipped her king over on its side. "Well played, Mr. Benning. You have a real knack for the game."

Jackson seemed to take the compliment well. "Don't sell yourself short. You're pretty clever yourself. Where did you learn to play like that?"

Elizabeth's face pinched inward for a moment, and Alex could swear that she was about to cry. After a second, she pulled herself together and then admitted, "Our late father taught me. He was an excellent player himself."

"I don't doubt it for one moment," Jackson said, clearly wondering about her reaction as well. "He certainly taught you well." It was as gracious as Alex had ever seen the man be.

Michelle pushed her cards into the middle of the table, showing that she was finished with their game, as well. Alex had to agree: it felt as though they'd been playing for hours.

"Is it getting cold in here," she asked, "or is it just my imagination?"

"It's a little chilly," Dutch answered. "Anyone mind if I start a fire?"

"A fire would be perfect," Alex said when no one protested. Dutch quickly had a blaze going, and the game afternoon had clearly come to a close.

Elise looked at her watch and then said, "If you'll all excuse me, I'd better get started on dinner."

"Need any help?" Michelle asked.

Jackson didn't like that at all. "You could burn a pot of water, Michelle. She doesn't need your help or your company."

"There, you're wrong," Elise said. "Michelle, I'd be delighted to have you come into the kitchen with me."

Michelle gave Jackson a superior look, and then she

joined Elise.

Dutch said, "If you all will excuse me, I'd better make the rounds of the cottages to make sure they're all secure before we get a real lashing later."

"I'll go with you," Alex said as he stood.

"There's no need," Dutch said. Was he angry with Alex's suggestion? "Harry never helps me. I can handle it myself, and there's no use in both of us getting soaked."

"I'm the innkeeper, so I have the final say," Alex said firmly as he grabbed a jacket. "Besides, we're on the buddy system, remember?"

"Suit yourself," Dutch answered as he got his jacket from the rack. "If we're going, let's get to it."

The rain was cold and stinging as it came down, and Alex immediately began to regret his decision to help the handyman make his rounds. Then Alex thought of how he hoped Harry would treat his inn back in Elkton Falls, and he knew that he'd made the right decision to come along. The wind was howling loud enough to make conversation difficult, so the two men walked from cottage to cottage in near silence, trying each door, making certain each window was locked and storm shutter closed.

At the far cottage where Jackson and Michelle had spent the night, the wind died, if only momentarily. Dutch took advantage of the lull and said, "That guy Jackson's some piece of work, isn't he?"

"What do you mean?"

"I was working next door, and he ordered me over here to fix the dresser in his cottage. He was complaining that one of the drawers was sticking, and I told him that we were beside the ocean. Wood swells, and things stick, and there wasn't a thing I could do about it."

"How did he handle that?"

Dutch grinned at him. "Not well. I was a hair's

breadth from giving him a black eye when Michelle showed up and smoothed over all of the ruffled feathers. She's way too good for him, if you ask me."

Alex just shook his head. He wasn't about to answer that, but it amazed him how some people seemed to bring out the worst in those around them.

As they finished their rounds, Alex was pleased when nothing appeared to be out of place. When they got to Dutch's little cottage on the way back to the Main Quarters, Dutch said, "I've been thinking about what you said. I've decided to move in with you into the main keeper's quarters after all. You might as well come on in with me. I want to grab a few things for tonight."

Alex readily agreed, eager to get out of the storm. He was pleased to see a large mat covering the scarred hardwood floor, and he stood on that as Dutch gathered a few essentials.

"Are you ready to go?" Dutch asked Alex after he was finished.

"In a second. There's something I want to ask you first while we're alone."

The handyman grinned at him. "I was wondering why you were so insistent on tagging along. You weren't concerned about the cottages at all, were you?"

"That's not true. I meant what I said," Alex answered. "But I've been wondering about something. Did you know Danvers before he came here yesterday?"

Dutch shook his head. "Nope, not a chance. He was an absolute stranger to me."

"So, he's never stayed here before?"

"That I can't swear to one way or the other," Dutch said. "The truth of the matter is that I never see most of the guests who come here to stay. My job is to make sure the plumbing works, that the cottages don't fall down before the ocean swallows them up, and that the lighthouse lantern is always full of kerosene and ready to light. I don't exactly interact with the paying customers at the inn."

"Is there really a chance the cottages are going to be underwater someday?"

"Not just a chance," Dutch said. "It's a certainty. Most folks, even ones from North Carolina, don't realize that the Outer Banks shoreline is changing all the time. Sand leaves one place and goes to another, and the shoreline is constantly changing. Why do you think they had to move the Hatteras Lighthouse? If they hadn't, the only way to get to it by now would have been by boat. In twenty years, this all might be gone. Not nearly as many folks care about Cape Kidd. It's not what you'd call picturesque, is it?"

"I don't know about that. I love the tower, whether it's odd red brick or not," Alex said. "That's part of its charm, if you ask me."

Dutch surprised him with a smile. "I like it, too. Let me tell you something. If you're ever stuck here in a hurricane, the lighthouse is the place to go. It's solid and stout, and it's the best chance you'd ever have to survive. Was there anything else, or should we rejoin our guests?"

"No, that's it," Alex said. He had no way to confirm or deny the truth of what Dutch had told him. The man told a plausible story, but he also could have had reasons of his own to want to see the private detective dead. Who knew what secrets might have driven Dutch to the isolation of a lesser lighthouse in a fairly inaccessible spot on the Outer Banks? He liked the man, at least when he'd been talking about the lighthouse, but folks Alex had liked in the past had still turned out to be killers on occasion. It was certainly no litmus test of innocence and guilt.

He'd have to keep his eye on the handyman.

Along with everyone else staying at the inn, as well.

Chapter 13

When they got back to the front porch of the main keeper's quarters, Alex saw that Greg Morrison was out there alone, sitting on one of the rocking chairs. He spoke up before Alex had a chance to. "Is everything okay out there?" he asked.

"So far, so good," Alex said, and then he turned to Dutch. "Why don't you go on in and get dry? You can store your things in back."

"Aren't you coming in, too?"

"I'll be there in a minute." This was the perfect opportunity to talk to Greg without his sister and brother around, and Alex wasn't about to miss the chance to interview him.

After Dutch went inside, Alex took the chair beside him as he said, "Wow, it's really coming down."

"Not much of a vacation spot, is it?" Greg asked. "No offense, but I doubt I'll ever want to come back here."

"Hey, why would that offend me? It's not my inn, remember?" Alex asked.

"Sure, that's right. It's easy to forget. You and Elise look pretty comfortable here. It's almost as if you belong."

"What can I say? We both have an affinity for lighthouses." Alex took a deep breath, and then he added softly, "I can't believe someone was murdered here. It's a shame Danvers was killed. He didn't deserve the ending he got, if you ask me."

Greg snorted. "You can't know that, though, can you? He could have been a real jerk who got what was coming to him and not merit your sympathy at all."

Alex stared at him for a second. "Wow, for a second there, you sounded as though you knew him."

Greg shook his head, clearly hoping to end that part of their conversation, but Alex wasn't about to let up. "Greg, I saw your face when you looked at that picture. You and your family were acquainted with him, weren't you?"

"You're crazy," Greg said, "and I don't have to sit here and listen to this." He started to get up, but Alex reached out and restrained him by grabbing his arm.

"Am I? How hard do you think the police are going to have to look to find a connection between the murder victim and your family?"

"Let them look," Greg answered. "We didn't do anything, and we certainly didn't kill him."

"Think about this, then. You have the chance to come clean with the rest of us right now. If you don't tell the truth, we're all going to tell the police that you hid it from us. Lying isn't exactly going to get you a free pass with the police. They're going to focus on the three of you, and the real killer might go free."

"Why would that bother me?" Greg asked. "Now I'm telling you to move your hand, or I'll move you myself, Alex. I'm going inside."

"That's a good idea," Alex said as they both stood. "Let's both go. I want to have a chat with your sister, anyway."

That appeared to scare Greg more than the threat of the police. "Don't say a word to her about our conversation. I didn't tell you anything."

"There, you're wrong."

Greg tried to grab Alex's arm this time before he could go inside, but he was too late.

Alex hadn't been bluffing. He walked into the inn and said directly to Elizabeth, "You might as well confess. Your brother just told me everything."

"You fool," Elizabeth spat out at her brother.

"He's lying," Greg pled.

Elizabeth's eyes narrowed as she looked back at

Alex. "Is that true?"

Alex simply shrugged. "I know you had a connection to Danvers. The only thing I'm not sure of is the degree to which you three knew him. I told your brother, and now I'm going to say the same thing to you. If you don't tell the rest of us how you're mixed up in all of this, we're all going to have to tell the police that you held out on us. How do you think that's going to look? Deny it all you want, but we saw your brother's reaction to that picture when he saw the dead man's face, and you were just a little too calm, and way too thorough when you examined the body this morning."

Jackson said, "He's right. You might as well tell us. After all, we told you our secret, and it can't be much worse than that."

"Michelle told us, to be more exact," Elizabeth corrected him.

Jackson waved a hand in the air. "What does it matter? The point is, we don't have anything to hide." He looked hard at her before he asked, "Do you?"

"I don't suppose you're going to stop pestering us until we tell you," Elizabeth said with a sigh.

John interjected. "Elizabeth, we're under no obligation to say anything."

"Let me handle this, John."

He let out a heavy sigh of exasperation. "Go ahead, do what you want. You're going to anyway."

His sister nodded, took a deep breath, and then she said, "Mr. Winston, you might as well grab a towel, dry off, and sit down. This might take some time to tell."

"Let me go get Elise first," Alex said. He hurried into the kitchen as he dried his hair on a towel by the door, and then he told Elise and Michelle, "You two need to come into the lobby right now."

"What happened? Did someone else die?" Michelle asked with a horrified expression on her face.

"No, the Morrisons are about to tell us their connection to Danvers, and I don't think you'll want to miss it."

"Let's go, Michelle," Elise said, and in another thirty seconds, everyone was gathered back in the lobby.

"Go on," Alex said as soon as everyone was in place, and Elizabeth Morrison began to speak. "We're ready to hear what you've got to say."

"Our father was a great many things," she began to say when John interrupted her.

"I've changed my mind. Elizabeth, this is none of their business," John said. "We don't owe them any explanations."

Elizabeth gave him a withering look. "John, I'm going to tell this whether you like it or not. Alex is right. The longer we keep this to ourselves, the worse it will look to the police. We knew Mr. Danvers, and there's no use denying it. Now, may I continue, or would you like to excuse yourself from this discussion?"

"I'm staying," John said softly.

"Pardon? I didn't hear you."

"I said I'm staying," John repeated.

Before Elizabeth would continue, she turned to Greg. "I assume you have no problem with this, since you're the one who brought it up."

"I keep telling you, I didn't tell him anything," Greg insisted.

Alex shrugged. "That's not entirely true. You said enough to get me suspicious."

Greg hung his head low, but he didn't try to deny it anymore. Elizabeth, to Alex's surprise, touched her brother's shoulder. "Greg, you have nothing to feel bad about. The more I think about it, the more I realize that we should have done this the moment we found the body."

Her brother looked up at her, but he still wouldn't meet anyone else's gaze. Elizabeth smiled softly at him, and Greg seemed to take great comfort in it.

"As I was saying," she continued, "we've known Mr. Danvers for the past seven months. He was the direct cause of our father's death, and none of us will ever forgive him for the role he played in his tragic end."

"What are you talking about?" Elise asked. "How did Danvers cause it? Did he actually kill your father?"

"No, but he may as well have put his hand on our dad's back and pushed him off that bridge in Wilmington. You see, he was never good with money. Let me amend that. He was good at making it; holding on to it was another matter entirely. He would never admit that he was in trouble, and if he needed help, the last thing he would have done was turn to us, though we would have been overjoyed to help him. You see, our grandfather could both earn *and* grow the money he made. He didn't respect our father's ability to handle money, so when our grandfather died, he left his estate in three equal portions, divided between the three of us."

"Cutting your dad out altogether," Jackson said. "That's some tough love."

Elizabeth looked at him harshly. "Actually, he thought he was saving him. If Father had to stand on his own, without family money to bail him out every time he lost his savings, Grandfather believed it would make a man out of him."

"As if he weren't already," John said.

"He was indeed," Elizabeth agreed. "I just wish we could have done something." The sadness in her voice was palpable.

"You shouldn't blame yourselves. He couldn't have asked you for help, even if he'd wanted to," Alex said.

"And why not?" Greg asked. "He knew we would give him whatever he wanted."

"That's just it. It was his father's money in his mind, forever, not yours. The last thing your dad would do if he had any sense of pride whatsoever would be to take that money after his father was dead. It wouldn't have been possible for him."

"He *was* a proud man," Greg said so softly Alex barely heard him.

"And that turned out to be one of his fatal flaws," Elizabeth said.

"I still don't see where the private detective comes into it," Michelle said.

Everyone looked at her and then at Elizabeth. "I'm just getting to that. The last time Father got in trouble, it was with someone else's money, not ours, and certainly not his. He 'borrowed' from a trust account he was supposed to be investing, and the investor began to suspect something was amiss. She hired Danvers to look into it, and he found the crime quickly enough. Father wasn't exactly skilled at hiding his tracks."

"The way you tell it, Danvers was just doing his job," Alex said. "Surely you can't fault the man for that."

"If he'd gone straight to the investor or even to the police with his knowledge, we could have lived with the outcome, no matter what. What he did instead was approach our father, demand payment for his silence, and then start applying more and more pressure until our father finally decided that there was no way out, so he jumped off that bridge in despair."

"How could you possibly know all of that?" Jackson asked.

Elizabeth explained, "He left his journal, and along with it, a suicide note on the last page. It told the whole sordid tale."

"So you wanted Danvers's head on a stick," Jackson

said, nodding in understanding. "It's understandable enough."

"And it will provide plenty of motive for the police," Elizabeth said. "That's why we decided to keep our involvement with the man quiet until we could figure things out for ourselves."

Something occurred to Alex. "You never planned to stay here at all, did you? You were stalking him even then, weren't you?"

Elizabeth nodded, but then she said quickly, "We had no intention of killing him. We've been tailing him for several weeks, showing up every time he was working on an investigation. We planned to keep dogging his steps until he broke down and begged us for our forgiveness."

Alex doubted a man hardened enough to be a private investigator would ever apologize for his actions, but he didn't really know the man. "But something changed."

"You're darn straight it did. Someone killed him," Jackson said.

"If I were you, I'd try not to look so pleased by that outcome," Elise said sharply.

Jackson shook his head. "I'm not glad the man's dead, but at least there are more suspects thrown into the mix now than the two of us."

Elizabeth shook her head. "But you just heard what I said. We didn't kill him. That wasn't our plan at all."

"Maybe you or your brothers got tired of being so passive," Jackson said. "It could be that one of you decided to end the cat-and-mouse portion of your plan and ramp it up to full-blown murder for revenge."

"Jackson," Michelle said reproachfully. "Don't speak to them like that. Apologize this instant for what you said."

Alex could see the wheels turning in Jackson's mind, and he knew that this could be a turning point in their relationship. It was clear that Michelle was coming into money. What wasn't clear was whether Jackson was willing to lick her boots to get his hands on some of it or not. After a moment or two of hesitation, he said, "I'm sorry. I'm just stressed out, I guess."

Michelle patted his arm as though he'd just done a special trick. "Thank you," she said softly. "I know how hard that must have been for you."

"You're welcome, my love," Jackson answered. It wasn't clear whether he'd done as he was told out of love or greed, but what was certain was that he was having trouble choking down his own pride in front of the crowd.

"So, it appears that we *all* need alibis for the time of the murder," Jackson said gently, careful to take any sting out of his words. Before Michelle could protest, he amended, "The police will want to know where we were last night. Michelle and I were together, so at least we're in the clear."

Alex coughed, and then said, "Not necessarily."

"What do you mean by that?" Michelle asked.

"One of you could have slipped out in the middle of the night, or you could have done it together. It's not pretty, but murder never is." Alex didn't like accusing any of his guests of murder, but the possibility had to at least be acknowledged.

"Alex, have you completely lost your mind?" Michelle asked, the hurt clear in her voice. "I thought you liked us."

He did indeed like Michelle, but he was willing to let the assumption that he felt the same way about Jackson slide. "How I feel about any of you has nothing to do with it. We're talking about murder here. All options have to be explored."

"At least I'm in the clear," Dutch said from the hallway.

"How do you get that?" John asked.

"Well, for starters, I'm the only one here who didn't

have a motive to kill the guy."

"At least that we know of," Jackson said, and Alex was surprised to see other heads nod in agreement as well. Were the five solid suspects trying to include the other three people at the inn as well to the mix?

"Hang on a second. Don't try to drag me into this," Dutch said angrily. "I'm just the handyman."

"That remains to be seen. Alex and Elise never met you until they showed up. Sure, there probably was a handyman here named Dutch, but what proof do we have that you are one and the same?"

"If I'm not Dutch, then where is the real man?" he asked.

Did he really expect anything other than the answer she provided? "You killed him, buried him in the sand, and took his place, waiting for your opportunity to strike out at Danvers yourself."

"I don't know what kind of twisted mind you've got, lady, but it's all complete and utter crap. I'm not a suspect."

"Until we learn otherwise, we're *all* suspects, including our hosts," Elizabeth said.

Alex answered, "We can deny our involvement just as much as the rest of you can, but what good would it do us? Neither Elise nor I had any reason to kill Danvers, but proving you don't know someone is harder than it might seem. In the end, we're just visiting here ourselves."

"That doesn't exactly clear you of suspicion, though, does it?" Jackson asked.

Elise shrugged. "I don't know how to convince you all that we're innocent or even if I should bother trying. What I do know is that I need to get started on making dinner."

Michelle started to join her as she walked to the kitchen when Alex saw Elise flinch a little. It wasn't at all clear that she wanted any company at the moment, especially from a murder suspect, which Michelle most certainly was now. Alex said, "Michelle, you should take some time to be with your...er...Jackson. Elise can handle things on her own."

Before she could protest, Alex trailed Elise into the kitchen. "Was that okay just now, or did I read your facial expression entirely wrong when you saw that Michelle was coming back here to help you?"

Elise looked startled to see him in the kitchen. "No, thanks for getting me out of that. Not that I don't love having you here with me, but shouldn't you stay in there and referee?"

"Frankly, I'd rather count the bricks in the lighthouse than deal with that group," he replied. "When it all comes down to it, you're the one I care about and the only one I want to be with. Do you mind the company?"

Elise kissed him, long and hard, and then she pulled away with a smile. "What do you think?"

"I think I'm glad I followed you in here just now," Alex said with a grin of his own.

Chapter 14

"What's on tap for tonight's meal? Any chance we can satisfy the vegetarians?" Alex asked her.

"I found spaghetti sauce in the pantry, but no pasta, if you can believe that," Elise said.

"It won't do us much good then, will it?"

Elise smiled. "Are you kidding? I've been dying to make homemade pasta for quite a while. What better opportunity?"

"It sounds complicated. Have you ever made it before?" Alex didn't doubt that Elise was more than competent in many ways, but he hadn't known this about her. The woman continued to surprise him, something he was perfectly fine with.

"My mother and I used to make it together all of the time when I was younger. The reason I suggested it was because I found this in the appliance pantry." She reached under the counter and pulled out a shiny chrome contraption the size of a tissue box.

"What does that do?" Alex asked. "Remember, we don't have electricity."

"We don't need it for this. It's all muscle power. You clamp it down like this," she said as she demonstrated, securing the machine on the edge of the counter, "and you take this handle and turn it."

"What happens when you turn it?"

"You feed the dough through, move this dial after each pass, and the sheets become thinner and thinner," she answered.

"What do you do when you get it down to the proper thickness?" Alex was skeptical, but he knew better than to question Elise's abilities in the kitchen.

"You use this extension," she said as she pulled another gizmo out, "to cut the noodles. Trust me, it will be great."

"We could make garlic bread, too," Alex said. "There are some loaves of French bread in the food pantry, since all the bread that I made is gone."

"That's your job, then," she said.

As Alex melted some butter on the stovetop and minced a little garlic to add to it, Elise measured out flour, a little salt, and got some eggs from the refrigerator. "It's stayed cold enough, but we'll probably have to finish what we've got left before long. At least the fridge wasn't fully provisioned, so not much will spoil."

"There's always that, though if this isolation lasts too long, we'll all be chewing on ice cubes," Alex said. As he kept an eye on the sauce in the pan while it continued to simmer, he watched Elise as she mixed the flour and salt together, then dumped it out onto the counter. Making an indentation in the middle of the flour, she cracked eggs and kept adding them until she was happy with the mixture. Taking her fork, she broke the yolks and then started adding more and more flour to the mix from the sides. It was an amazing thing to watch. She added a few drops of tap water to the mix, and only after she was satisfied with the consistency, Elise took a French rolling pin and went over the dough a few times until she had a nice thickness.

"What happens now?" Alex asked as he brushed the garlic butter on top of the diagonal wedges of bread he'd cut. After dousing each one, he placed it on a cookie sheet and put it into the oven he'd preheated.

"Now it's time to roll out the dough using the pasta maker."

Alex pulled out a seat and flipped it a half turn. As he did, she ran the dough through again. Only when she was satisfied with the texture of the dough did she move the rollers one step closer.

By the time she hit the seventh setting, the dough

was long, paper thin, and nearly translucent, not to mention a mile long. Using a knife, she cut the dough in sections, and then she added the cutting attachment.

"Are you sure I can't help?" he asked.

"This is the fun part. Tell you what. You can crank," Elise said. "I'll feed the dough and catch the noodles."

Alex took up his position, and under Elise's instructions, he began to turn the cutters. Thin, flat sheets of dough went in, and strands of newly formed pasta came out the other side.

"Is that all it takes?" Alex asked in wonder.

"That's it," she said, wiping her forehead with the back of her hand. Evidently making pasta might be simple, but that didn't mean that it still wasn't hard work. Elise had clean and dry dishtowels laid out on the counter, and as each batch of noodles made its way through the machine, she tossed them lightly onto the cloth, along with a little flour each time to keep them from sticking together. "We don't have a drying rack, so that's the best that we can do," she explained. "Is the water boiling yet?"

She'd instructed Alex to fill a large pot of water and start it boiling, which he'd done just after the garlic bread had gone into the oven.

"It's a rolling boil," Alex said. "We're good to go."

Elise looked at it, salted the water lightly, and then she added a little olive oil. She looked at Alex apologetically as she explained, "I'm not positive the oil helps to keep the noodles from sticking, but Mom did it, so that's good enough for me."

"Don't look at me. I'm just an observer."

"You're more than that," she said. "Alex, I can handle the rest here. Why don't you set the tables, now that we know everyone will be dining with us tonight."

"I put out plates, glasses, and tableware before," Alex said. "What else do we need?"

"Butter, grated Parmesan cheese, some salt and pepper, and that's it."

"It sounds like a simple meal, but I'd be hard pressed to come up with anything half as elegant even given twice the budget."

Elise laughed. "During tough times at the inn when I was a kid, we had beans and cornbread, and then we alternated that meal with pasta, but no sauce. I didn't even realize we were having it rough, it was all so delicious."

"It sounds to me as though you ate better than most," Alex agreed.

The innkeeper walked out of the kitchen and was surprised to find that two of the larger tables had been pushed together, making it more of a family style of dining.

Elizabeth looked at his curious expression and explained, "It's ridiculous for us to keep our distance. We're all in this together, so we might as well dine as a group. That is, if you don't have any objections."

"It's fine with me," Alex said, though what he'd really hoped for was a chance to eat alone with Elise in the kitchen. That clearly wasn't going to happen now.

After he finished tweaking the arrangement, Alex went back into the kitchen and found Elise pulling the garlic bread out from the oven. "That smells wonderful," Alex said. "Can I do that for you?"

She pointed to the sink. "Thanks, but I've got it. The pasta's drained, and the sauce has been heating on the stovetop. We're ready to eat."

Alex took the large platter filled with bread, and then after dropping it off at the large table, he came back for the sauce while Elise grabbed the pasta.

Once they were in the dining room, Jackson looked at the offerings. "Pasta? I hate pasta. Is that all you can feed us? You seriously can't do any better than that?"

Alex was about to say something sharp when Elise answered, "If you don't like it, and that goes for any of you, I'll do my best to make something else for you. After the rest of us eat, that is. There are limits to what we have available, and I won't have anyone squandering our meager supplies unless it's under my supervision. Is that understood?" There was no room in her statement for argument, and Alex pitied the guest who might be crazy enough to try.

"Jackson, it will be fine," Michelle said, and then she looked at Elise. "We appreciate all that you're doing under such trying circumstances."

There were nods around the table, and Elise took some pasta from the bowl and then passed it along while Alex ladled some sauce onto his own serving.

Jackson took two small forkfuls and placed them on his plate, added a lesser amount of sauce, and then took a bite. Alex watched his face as the tension eased instantly and a slight smile appeared. Jackson must have seen Alex watching him.

"You know what? It's not terrible," he said as he reached for the bowl again.

Elizabeth wasn't having any of that, though. "You had your turn. You can wait until we've had ours before you get a second serving."

She took a large portion, as did each of her brothers, but Elise had made more than enough for twice as many people, so running out was not a concern. The fare might have been simple, though delicious, but there was plenty of it.

To Alex's surprise and Elise's delight, by the time they were finished, there was barely enough pasta left to save.

It had been a big hit, and Alex was as proud of Elise as he could be. Not only had he chosen well in finding someone who complemented his abilities as an innkeeper, but he had found someone who truly made him happy. In the end, what more was there, really?

"What's on tap for tonight?" Michelle asked as Alex and Elise began gathering up the dirty dishes.

"I'm not sure. We could always play more games," Alex suggested.

"Isn't there anything else we can do?" Greg asked.

"Why don't you all go into the lobby and decide," Alex said.

"What are you going to do?" Jackson asked him.

"There's a great deal of cleaning up to do. You're more than welcome to join us if you'd like to lend a hand. That goes for any of you," Alex said, looking around the crowd.

"No thanks, I'll leave it to the experts. I'm not really big on pitching in," Jackson said.

Michelle gave him a troubled look before she offered, "I don't mind helping."

Elise smiled at her. "There's really not all that much. Alex and I do more than this at our inn every day. We'll be out shortly."

Michelle nodded in agreement, but Alex thought he saw a little disappointment in her expression. Was there trouble in paradise, and was the marriage that was valid only in spirit starting to collapse under the pressure of a murder? It wouldn't be the first relationship that suspicion had killed, he mused.

As they did dishes, Elise asked, "So tell me, Alex. Who do you think did it?"

Alex looked at her, startled by the question and pulled from his thoughts, which had been running along the exact same lines. "Pardon me?"

"Come on, I know you too well to think for one moment that you haven't been puzzling this out ever since you found the body. I want to know what you're thinking. I can't help you solve it if you won't confide in me."

He thought about denying it, but there was no use.

Elise knew him too well, if there was such a thing. "To be honest with you, at the moment, I like Jackson Benning or Elizabeth Morrison," he said.

"Why those two only?" she asked as she handed him another plate to dry. They often chatted as they did dishes together back at Hatteras West, but the subjects were usually more innocuous, like first kisses and favorite songs.

"Well, to start with, they both have strong wills and even stronger motives," Alex said.

"And they both have a knack for getting under your skin," Elise added.

"There's that," Alex said. "I suppose Michelle has more motive than Jackson to want to hide the truth of her affair, and either Morrison brother is just as capable of murder as their sister."

"So, that just leaves Dutch and the two of us as being free from suspicion," Elise said as she handed him another plate.

"Well, at least I know that *we* didn't do it," Alex said.

She must have read something in his statement. "What about Dutch?"

Alex thought about it a few moments before he spoke. "Elizabeth made a fair point earlier. How much do we really know about him, Elise? Harry told us about the handyman's presence in a letter, but that's it. He's a wild card, as far as I'm concerned."

"What do you mean? Alex, don't hold out on me."

Finally, he nodded his head. "I just can't get what Elizabeth proposed earlier out of my head. Elise, how *do* we know that he's the real Dutch? I doubt that's the name on the driver's license of the real man; it's an easy nickname to acquire. That means we can't identify him that way."

Elise nodded soberly. "And we can't just pick up the phone and ask Harry for a description. At the time, I discounted it as Elizabeth lashing out at anyone and everyone in sight, but now I'm having doubts myself."

Alex touched her shoulder lightly. "Elise, don't listen to me. I'm probably just being paranoid."

"As far as I'm concerned, if it keeps us alive, it's not being paranoid," she said. "I'm going to have to keep an eye on him."

"Why not? After all, we're already watching everyone else," Alex admitted. "I don't suppose it will hurt to keep tabs on Dutch, too."

"I don't like this, Alex. Being trapped with a murderer is more than we bargained for when we agreed to swap lighthouse inns," she said as she handed him the last plate and pulled the drain from the sink basin. They'd had to heat the teakettle on the gas stovetop to get enough hot water to wash the dishes, but it had cooled now. "I'm not afraid to admit it, but I'm scared."

Alex dried the plate, put it on the stack with the rest, and then threw the towel on the counter. "Trust me, I am, too. All we can really do is stay alert."

"I don't think I'll ever be able to get to sleep tonight," she admitted.

"I've been meaning to talk to you about that," Alex said. "I think it might be a good idea if we sleep in shifts."

She nodded. "Of course, that makes perfect sense. You *are* worried, aren't you?"

"You'd have to be crazy not to be," Alex said.

"Let's see. We run a lighthouse inn in the mountains. Don't you think that qualifies as a little over the edge anyway?" she asked with a smile, trying to lighten their moods.

"You're probably right, but what can I say? It's home."

Elise nodded, and he felt his heart swell again as she said, "I can't imagine ever being anywhere else."

Alex looked around the kitchen. "It's a shame there's no more work that needs to be done in here. I'm not all that eager to spend more time with these people."

"Maybe this will be the last night we have to," Elise said. "Surely someone will come dig us out of the sand tomorrow."

"I hope so," Alex said as he nodded in agreement, but in his mind, he added, "Before it's too late." He kept that part to himself, though. It wouldn't be good to alarm Elise even more than she already was.

But he doubted that he'd ever sleep again until they were safely back at Hatteras West.

Chapter 15

When Alex and Elise rejoined the others out in the
lobby, they found that the large leaf table that had been
against the wall was now open and had been pulled into
the center of the room. There were enough chairs for
everyone to have a seat. While the afternoon session of
games had been in smaller groups, it appeared that they
would all be playing together now. Outside, the wind
howled, and rain splashed up against the windows.
Candles were spaced around the table, illuminating the
scene with a flickering glow.

"What are we playing?" Alex asked.

"Anything but Clue," Michelle said.

"I can understand that," Alex agreed. It had been a
favorite of his family's when he'd been growing up, but
his brother, Tony, had won the vast majority of the
games. Alex long suspected his brother of cheating, but
then again, it might have just had something to do with
the fact the two had been enemies from the beginning of
their lives.

Greg added, "We thought that was a little too close
to home, anyway, given the circumstances. How do you
feel about Monopoly?"

"It's fine with me. Elise?" Alex asked.

"I should warn you that I'm not very good at it, but
why not?"

Jackson looked at her carefully. "You wouldn't be
sandbagging us now, would you?"

Elise shook her head. "No, but would it matter if I
were? After all, we're not playing for real money."

Jackson smiled. "Now, there's an idea. Just to
make things interesting, why don't we each put money
in the pot, and the winner takes all?"

"I'm not gambling," Elizabeth said.

"Come on. I'm not talking about high stakes here. Ten dollars each," Jackson pushed. "Even you can afford that."

"As a matter of fact, I could afford a great deal more, but I'm not about to waste my money on the likes of you."

Jackson shrugged. "That just shows a lack of confidence on your part. I was just trying to make things interesting."

"Don't you think things are interesting enough as it is?" Michelle asked him, clearly unhappy with his pushiness. She was definitely seeing her beau in a new light, one that was clearly quite a bit less flattering than the way she'd viewed him before.

Jackson didn't respond to her question, but he didn't look all that pleased that she'd asked it, either. He was on thin ice, and apparently he knew it.

As Alex retrieved the Monopoly game from the shelf full of games, he asked, "Who wants to be the banker?"

"You're the innkeeper," Michelle said. "You should do it."

"Fine. Elise, do you want to handle the properties?"

"I can't think of a reason why I shouldn't," she answered as she took the banded stack of properties from him. It was clear to Alex that Elise wasn't thrilled by the prospect of playing a board game with a murderer, and if he were being honest with himself, he wasn't all that excited about it, either. But in a skewed kind of way, it made sense. Keeping the killer at the table meant that no one else would die, as long as they were all around each other.

At least as long as the murderer stayed in the game.

In two hours, Elise, Greg, John, and Michelle had all been eliminated. Alex worried that they might wander off, but each of the losing contestants had their own favorite players still in the hunt, and there was really nothing else to do anyway, so, to his immense relief, the crowd lingered. As things stood at the moment, Dutch was in the weakest position, then Alex. The two heavyweights, Jackson and Elizabeth, were nearly equal. Jackson had more property, but Elizabeth had more cash. In short order, Dutch was eliminated, and then Alex, after he landed on Boardwalk, one of the few properties that Elizabeth owned. He stayed at the table as banker, and from his position, he had a close view of the two in combat. Was it really all that much of a coincidence that his two prime suspects were the only ones still standing?

"You go for the throat, don't you?" Elizabeth asked Jackson as he laughed with glee when she landed on St. James Place, a property he happened to have a hotel on.

As Jackson recounted the money she'd paid him, he said, "Life is a game, and games are like life. If you don't do everything in your power to win, why bother playing at all?"

Alex shot a quick look at Michelle, who was clearly startled by the man's attitude. Alex was willing to bet that she was seeing a side of him that he'd been careful to hide so far. No matter what happened, Alex was fairly certain that the marriage might not happen at all, regardless of the outcome at the inn. He wondered how they'd ever gotten together in the first place. Love could do strange things to people, he'd seen that as much as anyone, but when the smoke cleared, what was left was how two people related to each other and the world.

When the next turn came, Jackson landed on one of Elizabeth's properties. She took the money from him with barely a smile showing, and she added it to her carefully stacked rows without even counting it.

"You trust me that much?" Jackson asked her

incredulously.

"Why shouldn't I? After all, it's only a game," she answered.

Jackson seemed offended by the remark, and after that he tried his best to beat her, though now it was just down to who landed where and when.

In a long hour, with the lead changing hands a few times, Jackson had the bad luck to land on three of Elizabeth's few hoteled properties in a row, while she'd avoided his altogether.

Even Jackson could see the writing on the wall. He tipped his boot on its side as though he were playing chess and said heavily, "I concede."

Elizabeth offered a hand to him across the board, and for long moment, Alex wasn't certain that the man was going to take it. After Greg growled in the bottom of his throat, Jackson shook her hand, and then he quickly let it go.

"Come on, Michelle. Let's go to bed," he said as he stood.

Michelle shocked them all by saying, "No thanks, but you should go on by yourself. I'm going to stay up awhile."

Jackson clearly didn't know what to make of the mutiny, but he didn't argue the point, mainly because he was probably sure that he'd lose. Without another word, he grabbed one of the lit candles and made his way to the small room Alex had occupied the night before.

Elizabeth stood and stretched. "I'm afraid the day has left me quite weary as well."

She headed for her room, and her two brothers said good night in kind. The three of them were going to have a cozy night in the small space, but they'd asked for the accommodations, and Elise had unselfishly provided them.

Dutch said, "Honestly, I'm not a bit sleepy myself.

Is anyone up for another game of Hearts?"

They all agreed, and after they lowered the leaves of the table, the four of them sat and played well into the night. At one point, Jackson came out of his room with an angry expression on his face. "Are you coming to bed anytime soon, Michelle?"

"Not right now," she said, and he slammed the door when he got back to their room.

"He's not very happy, is he?" Elise asked her gently.

"He'll get over it, or he won't. Either way, it's not my concern. Do you happen to have another cot? I think it's cozier out here by the fire, anyway."

Dutch stood. "I'll go grab one for you."

Alex said, "Hold on. We're still on the buddy system, remember?"

Dutch nodded reluctantly, and the two of them went to the storage closet and got a cot, a sheet, a blanket, and a pillow with its case.

"I'm sure she's used to a whole lot better than this," Dutch said.

"We all are. It's only for one night, though."

"I hope you're right about that," Dutch said.

"Do you have any doubt they'll dig us out by tomorrow?"

He shook his head. "No, I'm pretty sure of it. They're good about taking care of us folks out here. Don't pay any attention to me. I'm just a little on edge."

"There you're in good company." Alex knew that the theory that Dutch was a killer was a possibility, but personally, he just couldn't see it. The man just seemed too genuine to Alex. Then again, he'd been wrong before.

By the time Alex and Dutch got back with the cot and bedding, the card game had been put away, and the table was back in its rightful place against the wall. "We hope you don't mind, but we decided that it's getting late," Elise said.

"It's fine by me," Alex replied. They divided the room in two, the men's cots on one side and the women's on the other, with the fireplace between them. Michelle fell quickly to sleep, but Dutch soon got up and started pacing around the room. "I'm coated with sand. I can't sleep like this. I need a shower."

"The water's freezing, remember?" Alex said.

"I don't care. I was outside in it a lot longer than you were today. Don't worry, I won't be long."

After Dutch went into the bathroom, Alex asked softly, "Elise, are you asleep?"

"No, I was afraid to nod off. Besides, I wasn't sure which one of us was going to stand guard first."

"I can take the first shift," he said. "Listen, before you go to sleep, I just wanted to apologize for getting you into this mess. I can't believe I dragged you all the way out here from Hatteras West just for you to risk your life."

"We're a team, Alex. I'll go wherever you go. You know that."

"I still feel responsible," he said.

"Did you kill that man?" she asked him softly.

"Of course I didn't," he replied. "You know that."

"I do. But unless you did it, you have nothing to apologize for. Alex, do you have a better idea now of who might have done it?"

He looked over at Michelle to see if there was a chance she was feigning sleep, but he doubted she would go so far as to snore to prove her point.

"My money's on Jackson right now," Alex said.

"Mine, too. He's got quite a temper, doesn't he?"

"And a killer instinct to boot," Alex agreed. "Did you see the way he looked at Michelle when she refused to go to their room?"

"I don't blame her for bunking out here with the rest of us."

"Neither do I," Alex agreed. "After what he said, I can see him killing to protect Michelle's money. I'm willing to bet that he already thinks of it as his."

"I'm worried for her safety, Alex."

"Don't worry. We'll keep an especially close eye on her," he said.

The bathroom door opened, and Elise said softly, "Good night, Alex."

"Good night."

Alex pretended to be asleep when Dutch came back into the room. The man quickly settled into sleep himself, and soon, Alex heard heavy breathing from all three of his bunkmates. The fire was dying, so he got up to add a few more logs to it, but that turned out to be his downfall. When the room had been chilled slightly from the cold, Alex could stay awake, but the added warmth, along with the stress he was under, put him to sleep before he had a chance to wake Elise to take her turn.

He was awakened the next morning by a scream coming from the bathroom area, and in an instant, Alex knew that his lapse of diligence had probably just cost someone their life.

Chapter 16

"What happened?" Elise asked as she came awake in the same moment Alex did. Michelle was stirring as well, but Dutch was sitting upright on his cot.

"I have no idea. I fell asleep," Alex admitted as he leapt out of his cot. He and Dutch rushed to the sound of the scream as Elise began to comfort Michelle. Alex was just as glad she'd stayed behind. If it was what he feared, he didn't want her to be with him when they found another body.

The two men discovered Elizabeth Morrison kneeling beside the shower, her gown wet from touching the damp tiles, and Jackson Benning's head cradled in her lap. Jackson was dressed in his pajamas, and the cord from his robe was knotted tightly around his neck. It wasn't a pretty sight, and Alex was glad that Elise hadn't come with him. Greg and John were trying to help Elizabeth up, but she was fighting them every step of the way.

"He might still be alive," she said as she searched for a pulse. "He's still warm, see?"

Dutch surprised Alex by moving him aside. "I took a first aid class a few years ago. Let me see what I can do."

The handyman knelt down beside Elizabeth, checked at the neck and wrist for a pulse, and then looked back at Alex as he shook his head. "I'm sorry. We're too late. He's gone. There's nothing we can do."

Elizabeth sobbed once, and then she laid Jackson's head back on the floor. She let her brothers help her stand, and once she was upright, Alex asked her, "What happened?"

"I came in to use the shower," Elizabeth explained through her tears. "I didn't want to wake my brothers, so I slipped out here without telling them. I reached behind the curtain to turn the shower on before I got in, but I heard an odd sound, as though the water was hitting something besides the tiles. I pulled the curtain back to see what it was, and there he was."

John stepped in and hugged his sister, with Greg patting her back. "There was nothing you could do for him," John said. "It was too late by the time you found him."

"I didn't care much for the man," Elizabeth admitted, her tears beginning to ease somewhat, "but I can't imagine who would hate him enough to kill him."

"Maybe he saw something he shouldn't have," Greg said. "If someone was trying to protect their secret, it might be reason enough to commit murder."

Alex himself had no problem imagining who might have done it. All three Morrisons had traded harsh words with Jackson the past day, none harsher than Elizabeth, and Michelle had her own reasons to want to be shed of the man. Even Dutch had had an altercation with him.

Once again, there were too many suspects and not enough clues.

"Somebody's got to tell Michelle about this," Alex said wearily.

"Tell her what?" Michelle said as she looked into the bathroom. With everyone else there, there was no real room for her to come all the way in herself, and Elise was standing just behind her in the hallway.

Alex tried to block Michelle's view of the body, but he wasn't able to do it in time. She saw the collapsed form of her boyfriend on the floor and shrieked once.

"Is he dead?" she asked through her sobs.

"I'm so sorry," Alex said as he tried to move her away from the door.

She held fast at first, but then Elise stepped in and

gave him a hand with her, putting her arm around the grieving woman. "Come on, Michelle. Let's go in the other room."

She allowed herself to be led away, and Alex was grateful for Elise's calming presence.

After the two women were gone, Alex looked at Dutch and the Morrisons. It was still a tight fit in the bathroom with all of them there.

"We need to close off this room," Alex said. "Let's go."

"It's a little late for that, don't you think?" Elizabeth asked, her gaze still glued to the body.

"What's already been done can't be helped," Alex replied. "We've already contaminated one crime scene. I won't let it happen again on my watch."

He expected a fight, but Alex was pleasantly surprised when they all filed out of the bathroom. They would be cramped in the main quarters for a while because of it, but that couldn't be helped. This body was going to stay exactly where it was. After they left the room, Alex locked the door with his key. He had no doubt that Dutch had a copy himself, but he couldn't worry about that at the moment. They'd have to use the restroom in the closest cottage, but it was a small price to pay.

Elizabeth turned to her brothers with firm resolution in her voice. "Grab what you need. We're leaving."

"We can't," John said. "You heard Dutch yesterday. The road is closed, and so is the beach. We'll never make it."

"That was yesterday. This is today. We're leaving."

"The police aren't going to like it," Alex reminded them.

"Maybe not, but I have no desire to lose a member of my family to whoever this maniac might be. We'll be safer taking our chances with the rough terrain."

Greg asked, "What about our luggage? We can't carry all of it through the sand."

Elizabeth looked at him fiercely. "Let me ask you something. Do you have *anything* you can't carry that is worth dying for?"

Greg shook his head.

Elizabeth added, "I didn't think so."

She turned to Alex. "You can try to stop us, but I'm warning you, you'll have a fight on your hands."

"I'm not going to do a thing," he answered. If they wanted to take their chances on the roads, he couldn't honestly blame them. "If for some reason you can't make it through, you're welcome back here tonight. I wouldn't wait too long, though. It could be tough finding us in the dark, and I can't imagine spending the night outdoors here, especially if it starts storming again."

"If you're trying to scare us, it isn't going to work. We'll take our chances with the elements," Elizabeth said. "John, do you agree?"

"I'm right behind you, sis," he said.

They all walked out into the lobby, and Elise asked them, "What's going on?"

"The Morrisons have all decided to check out," Alex said.

"That's an unfortunate expression given the circumstances, don't you think?" Elizabeth asked him.

"Sorry. I meant to say that they are leaving the inn."

"Then the roads are finally open?" Michelle asked hopefully.

"No," Alex said firmly. "At least not as far as I can tell."

"My sister makes a good point," John said. "It's too dangerous staying here at the inn any longer than we have to. Michelle, you're more than welcome to join us, if you'd like."

Alex expected her to agree when she surprised him. "I don't think it's a good idea for any of us to go," she said firmly. "I'm staying right here. I trust Alex and Elise."

"With your life?" John asked.

"Yes," she replied, but Alex noticed that it lacked some of the confidence it had earlier. "Besides, Dutch is staying, too. Aren't you?"

She turned to look at him, and the handyman answered with a smile. "There's no place I have to be but right here."

"You're making a grave mistake, young lady," Elizabeth said.

"Not as big as the one you might be making," Michelle answered.

Elizabeth turned to Elise and said, "You know you're welcome to join us as well."

"Thanks, but I'm staying, too. I go where Alex goes," she said simply, and he felt his heart skip a little faster at the sound of it.

"You know what my answer is. I'm staying," Alex replied. "This might not be my inn, but I'm responsible for it, and I won't just abandon it, no matter what the circumstances might be."

Elise nodded her approval, but John looked at them both as though they were crazy. "It's your funeral. Strike that. It's your decision. That's what I should have said."

"Elise," Elizabeth asked, "would it be possible to get some bottles of water before we go?"

"Sure. We've got plenty of those in the storage room," she answered after first waiting for Alex's nod of agreement. They were a team, and neither one of them was afraid to consult with the other if it was needed. The water was a resource, but fortunately, they did indeed have plenty to spare.

After the Morrisons took two bottles each, Elizabeth

turned to Alex and said, "I'd love to say that it was fun, but we both know that I would be lying."

"I just hope you know what you're doing," Alex said.

"Given the circumstances, I really don't see that we have any choice."

After the three of them were gone, Dutch pulled Alex aside and asked softly, "Should I follow them?"

"You're leaving too?" Alex asked, shocked by the man's sudden change of heart.

He shook his head. "That's not it. I just want to make sure they don't double back and try to get rid of us, too. Once I'm sure they're on their way, I'll come straight back."

Michelle looked frightened. "Do you think it's possible they'd come back for us?"

"It could happen, and it's easy to prevent, so why not keep an eye on them?" Dutch suggested.

Alex nodded. "I'm not sure that's a bad idea at all," he said. "Are you sure you want to do this?"

"I'm positive. I'll see you later." As Dutch headed out, he said, "I wouldn't mind taking a few of those waters for myself. It might be a long walk."

Elise got them for him, and Dutch left the inn.

Five minutes later, Michelle said, "Something just occurred to me."

"What's that?" Elise asked.

"What if *Dutch* is the killer? Could we have just given our blessing for him to hunt the Morrisons down and pick them off, one by one?"

"But he had no beef with Danvers," Alex said.

"That we know of," Michelle reminded him.

Elise asked, "Would you two mind moving this discussion into the kitchen? I thought I'd get an early start on lunch."

"Do you think we'll be here that long?" Michelle

asked. "Surely someone will come get us today. I'm too spooked to stay here another night, if you know what I mean."

Alex said, "I wouldn't be at all surprised if the police are here by dusk. I heartily doubt that we'll have to spend another night at the inn."

The relief on her face was clear. The strain of the last few days was wearing on her, replacing her once-ready smile with a constant worried frown.

Elise must have noticed it, too. "Come on, Michelle."

As their guest followed her, Elise turned back to Alex. "Are you coming?"

"It's a little chilly in here," he said. "I thought I might get a fire started while you two work on lunch."

"Excellent idea. We'll keep the doors propped open so we can hear you, and then we can have a picnic out here in front of the fire."

After the women were gone, Alex started laying the fire and thinking about the folks who'd just left. It was true that the Morrisons had a beef with Danvers, but what could have caused them to kill Jackson? Had he seen one of them do something incriminating, like leaving the man's cottage after the murder? The three of them had barely left each other's company since they'd arrived, so it was unlikely that one of them could commit murder without the other two knowing about it. Loving family was one thing; conspiring to cover up two murders was something else altogether. Elizabeth Morrison was strong, there was no doubt about that, but just how forceful a grip did she have on her brothers' lives? He could understand Greg going along with her on just about anything, but John had shown real spirit from the beginning. Alex couldn't see him hanging for his sister, no matter how much he loved her.

Then there was Dutch. Could he have killed both men? Alex wasn't sure why, but he had a feeling in his gut that the man was exactly what he seemed to be, no matter what Elizabeth had suggested. In Alex's paranoia, he had wondered aloud if Dutch was really Harry and Barbara's handyman, but he knew that chances were good that the man was exactly as he seemed. After all, he'd known about the radio, hadn't he? That showed at least a rudimentary working knowledge of how the inn was run.

That left Michelle. She was so passive that it was difficult to imagine her in the role of murderer, no matter how hard he tried. Still, he couldn't rule her out.

The more Alex thought about it, the more likely each of his suspects became in turn. He was certain he could talk himself into believing that *any* of the folks around them had committed the murders.

And then another thought struck him. What if the two murders weren't tied together? Could there have been two separate killers loose at the lighthouse? He knew that the odds were good that just one person was a murderer in such a small group of people, but that didn't mean that it was impossible.

It brought up a new and entirely unwelcome train of thought, and he was still considering it when Elise came in.

"Alex, is something wrong? I thought you were going to start a fire."

He looked up to find Elise staring at him.

Alex shrugged. "Sorry about that. I was just thinking about what a mess we're in," he answered.

She rubbed his shoulder lightly. "Why don't you start the fire and we'll have that picnic I promised? Come on, it will be nice."

He wasn't sure how good it could be, but Alex didn't want to do anything to extinguish the hope in Elise's eyes.

"That sounds great," he answered as he lit the match he'd been holding in his hand.

The wood was dry, and the fire leapt into quick flames. Alex rubbed his hands together in front of it and asked, "Where's Michelle?"

"She wanted to help, so I let her make the sandwiches." Elise frowned as she added, "I'm a little afraid for the Morrisons and Dutch. What if they don't make it?"

"They can always come back here," Alex said. "And if they do get out, they can send help. I'll feel a lot better once this is all over."

"I will, too. Once we get back to Hatteras West, I don't think I ever want to leave it again."

"That sounds good to me."

Michelle brought out a tray stacked with sandwiches, more than the three of them could ever eat. Her gaze shifted to the back bathroom where Jackson's body remained, but Alex watched as she forced down the emotion and did her best to put on a happy face. "Sorry, I got carried away. Could someone grab the sweet tea and glasses?"

Elise started to when Alex said, "I'll do it. You enjoy the fire."

Alex got the other tray, and the three of them ate in front of the fire.

After they were finished, Michelle asked, "What's next?"

"We've got a little cleaning up to do," Elise said. "The place is a real mess. There are cots to put away, and floors to sweep."

Odd. Alex had no intention of working as an innkeeper while things were so uncertain, but in his heart, he knew that Elise was right. As soon as they were out of there, they wouldn't be back, and it wouldn't be fair to leave more work than they had to for Harry and Barbara on their return.

"Can I pitch in?" Michelle asked.

Alex was about to agree when Elise said, "You

mentioned walking along the beach while we were in the kitchen. Maybe you can find some pretty shells. After the storms we've been having, I bet they are everywhere."

"Oh, that sounds nice," she said as her gaze shifted to the back again. It was clear what she wanted most in the world was to get away from the body of her former boyfriend. "Thank you for the suggestion. Can I at least help clean up lunch?"

"You made the food. We'll do it," Elise said.

As soon as Michelle was gone, Alex asked, "What was that all about?"

"I know she means well, but Michelle has been underfoot all morning, and she's driving me a little crazy. She loves seashells, so why shouldn't she get a little vacation out of this? Besides, it's not like she has to worry about a killer stalking her. Everyone else is gone. It's got to be torture being so close to Jackson's body. Did you notice how she kept glancing back at where it was? I figure she'll be safe enough on her own now."

"If they didn't backtrack, that is," Alex said.

"Dutch is watching out for that, remember?"

He nodded. "I know, but what if that story was just a ruse of his so we'd drop our guard? Dutch may have had no intention of following the Morrisons, and he could be out there somewhere waiting to pounce. Forget it. I'm being too paranoid."

"Or just the right amount," Elise said. "Come on."

"Where are we going?"

"We have to stop her before she's in danger."

Chapter 17

Fortunately, Michelle hadn't gone far. The pounding of the surf was so loud it obscured their voices when they called out to her, and as Alex and Elise approached her, she looked up at them, so startled he half expected her to bolt straight into the ocean to get away from them.

"It's just us," Alex said as he and Elise hurried up to her.

"You were right, Elise. The shells are magnificent. I thought you two were going to clean the inn."

Alex lied, "We were, but searching for shells sounded like more fun to us, too."

Michelle wasn't buying that, though. "You were worried about me, weren't you? Go on, admit it."

"Maybe just a little," Elise said.

"As much as I appreciate your concern, I'm a big girl. I can take care of myself. Go back and do your work. I'll be fine."

"We don't mind, really," Elise said.

Michelle frowned. "I don't know how to put this delicately, but I'd really like a little time to myself. Is that okay?"

"Of course it is," Alex said as he took Elise's hand in his. "Take your time. We'll see you back at the inn."

As they walked back to the lighthouse, Elise said, "She needs time away from *me*? You've got to be kidding me."

Alex laughed. "It's hard to imagine, isn't it? I for one can't get enough of you."

She smiled. "I know, I should be thankful for every moment we get. Come on, let's clean some rooms."

"You know all the right things to say," he answered.

For obvious reasons, they skipped Danvers's cottage

and Dutch's as well, but that still left plenty of work to do. "Should we split up?" Elise asked. "We can get more work done quicker that way. These cottages are so small, we'll keep bumping into each other if we try to clean them at the same time."

"I'm willing to risk it if you are," Alex said. "But the truth is, I don't want to separate."

"I don't, either. We'll deal with the tight quarters. Which cottage should we tackle first?"

"The three Morrisons'," Alex said. "We can pack their bags and keep them at the front desk until they come back for them."

They had changed the sheets and were making the bed in Elizabeth Morrison's cottage when Alex stepped on something.

He leaned over and picked it up from the floor, and Elise asked, "What is it?"

"A small piece of ammunition," Alex answered. "Elise, it looks as though she's armed."

"She has a gun?" Elise asked, nearly losing her composure. "Why didn't she tell us about it?"

"Maybe she was afraid that it might look bad for her if we knew," Alex admitted.

"What should we do, Alex?"

"The first thing we need to do is search this place from top to bottom and make sure it's still not here," Alex said.

After a brief but thorough hunt, they knew the gun was gone. Alex guessed, based on the size of the ammunition, that it was a small-caliber handgun.

"We have to warn Dutch," Elise said as she dropped the old sheets in the corner. They'd brought fresh linens and had put them on the dresser for later.

"How are we supposed to do that? I have no idea what direction they took, and there's no way we'd ever catch them. They've had too big a head start."

"You're right," Elise said. "Why didn't she bring the gun out after we found the first body? She could have used it to protect us, and poor Jackson might not be dead."

"The question is, who would she be protecting us from? Herself, or one of her brothers? I doubt she'd be on our side if one of them is the murderer."

Elise frowned. "One victim was struck from behind, while the other was choked, again, probably from behind. No bullets were used, but we seem to have ourselves a sneaky killer. They had to get pretty close to both victims before they could strike."

"Clearly, then, it was someone both people trusted," Alex said.

"And didn't consider a threat," Elise amended.

"So, everyone's on the list again. I'll be honest with you; I wouldn't mind having a way to protect ourselves at the moment, even if Michelle is the only one around." Alex glanced around and then added, "That we know of."

Elise shook her head. "Maybe it's better that we're not armed. It wouldn't do to start shooting at shadows. Let's finish these rooms. We can talk while we work."

"Don't we always?" Alex asked. He put the bullet in his pocket and kept an eye open for any other clues that might pop out at them. No one knew guests better than the people who cleaned their rooms, and Alex had learned more than he'd care to admit during his tenure as the innkeeper at Hatteras West.

There were no more surprises in Elizabeth's cottage, though.

John's and Greg's cottages were both lacking in any clues at all, and they added nothing to the information Alex and Elise had amassed so far.

Alex then headed for the cottage Michelle and Jackson had shared, but Elise put a hand on his arm. "We shouldn't go in there."

"Why not? Their things are gone, and Jackson's body is back at the inn."

"I don't want to have to tell the police we were snooping," Elise admitted. "What if they call Sheriff Armstrong back home to check up on us? Can you imagine what he'd say if they ask him about us?"

Alex shook his head. "Nothing too pleasant, I'm sure. So then, we're finished, aren't we?"

"For now. Let's go back and clean the kitchen, and then we can figure out what we should have for dinner."

"I was honestly hoping we'd be gone by then," Alex admitted.

Elise shrugged. "I'm guessing we're going to have to spend one more night here, whether we like it or not. I'd better see what I can scrounge up for dinner. Michelle isn't going to like being trapped here another night."

"She'll have to get in line," Alex said. "It's pretty clear that we're not particularly thrilled about it, either."

They found Michelle waiting on them on the front porch, as though she were afraid to go back into the main keeper's quarters by herself. The last few days had been quite a strain on her, and Alex could see a haggard expression in her eyes.

"We're not getting out of here tonight, are we?" Michelle asked as she looked around at the growing shadows.

"I don't think so," Alex said.

"Did the Morrisons make it out? Why hasn't Dutch come back?"

"I wish I knew the answer to either one of those questions," Alex said.

"I just want this all to be over," Michelle said.

Alex knew he had to do something to lift her spirits a little. "Tell you what. Why don't you help Elise in the kitchen, and I'll get that fire stoked up again."

"Okay. That sounds good to me," Michelle said,

though it was clear she'd rather be anyplace else in the world than there.

"Come on," Elise said. "Let's go see what we can come up with."

After they were gone, Alex started collecting more wood from the covered front porch. As he did so, he realized that he needed to rethink everything he'd learned so far about the murders. The first and most important item was the clue they'd gotten from Danvers's room.

M w/ B. M 2?

He'd been thinking about it off and on ever since they'd first found it on the inside of that matchbook cover. It could have meant many things, but there wasn't a D there, so he thought that without more evidence, Dutch most likely wasn't the killer. His true first name might start with an M, but wouldn't the detective put "Dutch," since that was how the man was known, regardless of his given name?

M w/ B.

The first part most likely meant Michelle with Benning. It wasn't unusual to use a woman's first name and a man's last while making a quick note. If Danvers had indeed been trailing the pair, it would make sense that his note would be a reference to them.

But what about M2? Could that somehow represent the Morrisons? There were three of them though, not two, so it just didn't fit.

And then Alex really tried to take a fresh look at the last guest still at their inn.

M2? could be the private detective's speculation that Michelle might be hiding more than it initially appeared. M2 could mean that he thought Michelle could be capable of her own acts of evil. Could Alex and Elise be stranded at the inn with the real killer after all?

The more he considered it, the more Alex realized that it started to make sense. After all, Michelle had the best motive there was to stop Danvers and then, later, to kill Jackson. The private detective could have kept her from the money she was going to get in the divorce settlement, and her supposed boyfriend had shown a side of greed and cold-hearted behavior that she might never have seen before. Jackson could have easily done his best to take her money once she got it, most likely through blackmail. Then why hadn't Alex seen all of that before? It was one of his true blind spots. He wanted to believe the best in people, and Michelle had presented a sympathetic front to them. No, it was more than that. She'd portrayed herself as a passive victim ever since she'd arrived at the inn, nearly always deferring to those around her.

Except when it mattered to her.

Could it be true? There was just one way to find out. If Alex didn't solve this before the police arrived, she might never be caught.

Chapter 18

There was only one way to find out. As dusk began to approach, Alex knew that he had to lay a trap for Michelle, and if she took the bait, he'd know that his reasoning had been right. If she didn't, then most likely one of the Morrisons had murdered both men.

It was time for Alex to manufacture a little evidence of his own and see what happened. He took an old piece of paper that Harry used in his files, scribbled something illegible in pencil on it, and then smeared it with his finger to make it even more unrecognizable.

When he walked into the kitchen, he held the paper up to show Elise and Michelle. "I just found something in Jackson's pants pocket," he said excitedly. "This was folded up and sitting on his bed."

Elise put down the knife she was using to chop vegetables. "Why were you examining the room alone, Alex?"

"I had to know if there was anything we missed," he explained. There hadn't been time to clue Elise in on his plan, and besides, if she didn't know what he was up to, she wouldn't be able to give him away accidentally.

Elise seemed to take that in. "Okay, I suppose that I can understand that. What did you find?"

Alex was beginning to feel really guilty about lying to her. He hated not including her in his ruse, but there had been no way to get her away from Michelle, so he really didn't have any choice. He would apologize later. Right now, he needed her to be convincing in her belief.

"Yes, what does it say?" Michelle asked.

Elise put the knife in her hand down on the counter. "Hang on a second. I want to know, too, but Alex, you really shouldn't have gone in there without the two of us."

"I'm sorry," he said. "I wanted a chance to look around by myself, and I'm glad I did. What if the killer found this and destroyed it before we ever saw it? If that happened, there wouldn't be any evidence left at all." As he spoke the last words, he looked straight at Michelle.

"You never answered my question," Michelle said. "Haven't you read it yet?"

"I can't make out all of it," he said, "but what I've read so far appears to be about you. Danvers's name is mentioned, too."

She frowned. "It's natural that Jackson would write me a note about the detective. Perhaps he had a thought on who might have killed the man. I'm sure you've misunderstood what he wrote. Let me see it. I can read his sloppy handwriting. I'll be happy to interpret it for you."

When Alex balked at the suggestion, she repeated, "I'm not kidding. Let me have it, Alex."

He knew if he handed it over, his game, and any chance he had of proving that she was a double murderer, would be over.

"If it's all the same to you, I think I'll hold onto it for now," Alex said. "I'm willing to bet that the police will be interested in seeing it."

Michelle looked as though she were going to cry, and Elise's natural reaction was to offer her comfort.

It might have been her last mistake though, as Michelle grabbed the knife and held it against Elise's throat the moment she was within reach.

It happened so quickly that Elise could do nothing but gasp as the steel edge nicked her neck.

"I'm going to ask you one last time, Alex. Give me the note," Michelle said, any softness now completely absent from her voice.

Gone was the soft, vulnerable tone usually heard in her voice, replaced by a wicked, cold delivery. Alex could certainly see this version of the woman as a murderer. He just hoped he hadn't erred so badly that Elise would have to pay for his failure to judge the woman correctly in time.

If Alex could buy a little time, maybe he could find an opening to save Elise. One thing he was certain of, though. If Michelle read that fake clue, they would both be dead. At that point, he doubted that a few more murders would matter to Michelle one way or another. "Let me get this straight. You killed Danvers to keep him from reporting your behavior to your soon-to-be-ex-husband, but why kill Jackson? Was he going to blackmail you for a cut of the money after you tried to dump him?"

"Have you been listening in on my conversations?" she asked with a snarl. "It's either that, or you're very good at guessing."

"I kept playing things over in my mind, and there was only one connection between Jackson and Danvers that made sense, and that was you."

"The Morrisons had reasons of their own to want the PI dead," she said.

"Maybe so, but Jackson was another case altogether. Killing him here was where you made your mistake," Alex answered. He tried to reassure Elise with his gaze, but the look of terror in her eyes was unmistakable. He had to do something, and quickly, if she was going to have the slimmest chance of surviving the attack.

"Come on," Michelle said with a laugh. "Jackson had a way of agitating people by his very nature. He could have pushed *any* of them until they snapped. At least that's the way I'm going to explain it to the police."

Alex shook his head. "It doesn't wash, and the cops will see that, too. You have one choice, Michelle. You can try to get away, and Elise and I won't stop you. Who knows? If you get a big enough head start, you might just escape."

"The roads are closed, remember?" she said, not bothering to deny his accusations anymore.

"You can take my truck. You could probably get through," Alex said, though he doubted she would get very far in the sand.

Michelle shook her head, and Alex saw the knife blade draw blood from Elise's neck. "Nice try, but you're not in any position to dictate my behavior. What is it with you men? Do you think of all women as helpless little creatures you need to order around, or worse yet, protect? That was the trouble with Malcolm. My unfortunate husband thought he could save me, the poor thing, and when he finally realized that he couldn't, he tried to throw me away. I didn't go cheaply, though. With his divorce settlement, I won't have to worry about money ever again."

"He wasn't smart enough to get a prenup?" Alex asked.

She laughed, a sound that sent shivers down Alex's spine. "The fool was in love, and I decided to make him pay for it. Danvers was going to blow that, so he had to go. He didn't even dream that I'd ever come after him, can you believe that?"

"No, I don't," Alex said. "I think that's what the matchbook was all about. He wrote a note that you were with Benning, but that he had to watch you, too. That's what the 'M2?' entry meant; I'd bet my life on it."

"You may not realize it, but you already have." She shrugged. "Keep your note. I'll take it off your dead body later. I was willing to pay Danvers off, but he tried to extort most of the money I'd get in my divorce! It turns out that was the man's pattern, but I didn't know it at the time. He made the mistake of turning his back on me, and I saw an opportunity, so I took it."

"It didn't end there, though, did it?" Alex asked her.

"That still doesn't explain the second murder."

She looked at him with distaste before she answered, "Jackson saw me leaving Danvers's cottage right after I killed him. He demanded to know what had happened, so I showed him. After that, Jackson told me that one way or the other, he was going to get half my money, but I never gave him a chance to tell me how he planned to do it. It was amazing how easy it was to twist that sash around his neck until he couldn't breathe. He fought hard, but it was no use. I was too strong for him."

"Okay, you win," Alex said, knowing this was his chance. "Here's the note."

It was time to act, do or die. He started to hand it to Michelle. If he could get her to drop her guard for a second, he'd throw himself onto the knife if it meant giving Elise a chance of getting away.

She wasn't going to do it, though. "Throw it on the cooktop."

He did as he was told, and as Michelle turned the burner on, he saw her grip ease ever so slightly on the knife against Elise's neck. Alex reacted, not even thinking about what he had to do. He threw himself at Michelle, grabbing at her hand with the knife. She instinctively lunged at him, and he felt the blade bite deep into his belly.

"Run!" he yelled at Elise, but she wasn't about to desert him. Instead, she grabbed a nearby pan and swung it at Michelle's head with all she had.

Michelle must have sensed it, though, because she moved at the last second, and the weapon glanced off without doing any real harm. The murderer grabbed a cast iron skillet of her own from the rack above the island and looked at Elise as though she were already dead.

Alex pulled the knife blade out, and he couldn't help crying out in pain as he did so. Elise looked at him for an instant, something that very well might have been her last mistake. The skillet connected with her skull, and she went down in a heap on the floor.

Alex was on the ground beside her, and the blood was seeping from his wound. Michelle considered them for a moment. She was reaching for the knife to finish them off when Alex heard something banging from the lobby.

"Give up," he croaked. "The police are here."

"You'd better pray it's true, but it's probably nothing. One of the shutters probably came loose again." She stared hard at him. "If there's a chance your girlfriend is still alive, you'll keep your mouth shut, or she'll surely be dead when I get back."

All that Alex could do was nod numbly.

The second Michelle was out of the kitchen, he crawled over to Elise, holding one hand over his torso wound to staunch the blood flow as much as he could.

"Elise? Can you hear me?" Tears obscured his eyes as he stared at her, praying for a single sign that she was still alive.

She didn't move, and Alex thought he was going to die.

As he continued to cry silently, Alex at last saw her stir.

"Alex?" she asked softly. "Are you okay?"

He touched her face lightly. "Elise, can you stand up? We need to get out of here."

"I think so," she said as she pulled herself up. "My hair must have softened the blow. You're really hurt," she added as she stared at his bleeding stomach.

"It's not that bad," Alex said. "Can you help me up?"

"You shouldn't move," Elise said, her words slurring a bit. How hard a hit had she really taken?

"If we don't go right this second, we're both dead. Come on, Elise. You can do it."

With her help, he somehow managed to stand, though he was in great pain. Grabbing a dish towel, he pressed it against the wound in his stomach. The pain ratcheted up another level, but he managed to take it.

"Where can we go?" Elise asked. "She'll find us."

"If she does, she does, but Elise, if we're going to die anyway, we'll do it fighting. We need to get inside the lighthouse."

A plan was forming in his mind. They were in no position to ambush Michelle given their injuries. Between Alex's deep wound and Elise's probable concussion, flight was the only option they had.

As Alex led her out the back door, Elise asked, "Why are we going in there?"

"It's the only door we can lock that she can't break down. It was designed to withstand a hurricane."

Elise nodded. "If we have to die, I'd rather it be there, anyway." Resignation was thick in her voice.

"Don't give up yet," Alex said. "I have an idea."

"I hope it's a good one," she said, and they stumbled out together into the growing night.

After they were inside the lighthouse, Alex told Elise to lock the door.

"Do you really think that's going to stop her?" she asked him.

"It might slow her down, and that could be all we need."

"What now?" Elise asked once that was accomplished.

It was time for part two of his desperate plan. "We go up."

"Can you do that? I'm not sure that I can," Elise said wearily.

"We have to find a way."

"Okay. You can lean on me if you need to."

"We'll lean on each other," Alex said, fighting

another wave of pain.

As they started to climb the first steps together, there was a pounding at the door.

"I know you're in there," Michelle screamed. "Let me in."

"No," Alex shouted. It was clear that the police weren't coming to their rescue. He was losing blood despite the compress, and Elise was disoriented from the blow. Things looked bad for the two of them.

"Can you make it up to the top of the stairs?" Alex asked her.

"Maybe. Can you?"

"With your help," he answered with a grin. Outside, there was a more regular pounding now, and Alex figured Michelle was using the axe to break her way in. As he and Elise stumbled up the stairs, he said, "At least this lighthouse isn't as tall as ours."

"I'd never make it up all of the steps of Hatteras West," Elise said.

When they finally got to the top, Elise looked around in vain. "What good did this do us, Alex?"

"We have to light the beacon lantern," he said as he fumbled with the matches on a shelf beside the lantern.

"What good is that going to do? It won't stop her."

"No, but it will tell everyone within sight where we are," he said, and then added with a weak smile, "Besides, our neighbor threatened to call the police if we lit it again. Can you think of any better reason?" After the matches slipped out of his hand again, he said, "I'm sorry. You'll have to do it."

Elise retrieved them, and then she lit the mantle of the lantern. After she hung it in place, she moved back to Alex, who had slumped down against the brick side.

"Hang in there," she said.

"Elise, there's something you should know," he said, and then he began to choke. Had Michelle hit something more vital than muscle when she'd stabbed him? How much longer did he have?

"Alex, save it for later. We'll get out of this."

"I don't think so. Not this time. You know that I love you," he said.

"I love you, too," she answered as she began to cry.

As he slumped down, Alex said, "I was going to ask you to marry me."

They both were crying now as he asked, "What would you have said?"

"I would have said yes," she answered, sobbing for a moment herself. "Alex, I don't want it to end like this."

"I'm beside you, in a lighthouse, with a lit beacon," Alex rasped out the words. "There are worse ways to go."

"You're not getting off the hook that easily," Elise said. "You made a promise to me, and I'm going to see that you follow through with it."

"There's nothing left that we can do now," Alex said.

Elise kissed him quickly but firmly. "My head's starting to clear a little, and I have a new reason to want to survive this. We're not finished yet, Alex."

That's when they both heard the door below them crash open.

A few seconds later, they heard Michelle run up the stairs toward them.

Chapter 19

Elise stood quickly, and Alex watched her as she took the lantern from its hook. "How will they know we're here if you take the light out of the prism?" he asked, his voice getting weaker and weaker.

"It's time for Plan B," she said, the newfound resolve thick in her voice.

"I didn't realize that we even had one of those," Alex said softly, but he wasn't at all sure she'd heard him.

As Michelle neared the top landing, she called out, "That noise we heard before was just the wind. No one's going to rescue you. I was going to kill you both quickly as a favor, but that's out now. You're going to pay for making me chase you down like dogs."

As she neared the top step, Alex saw that Elise was pulling the lantern back to strike out at Michelle.

The only problem was that she'd be able to see it coming.

He had to do something.

Screaming out in pain, Alex lunged for Michelle himself, despite his wound. She still had the fire axe in her hands, but his action startled her so much that she must have forgotten what she was holding. In the second Michelle lost her focus, Elise brought the lit lantern down on her head. She struck Michelle with such force that the glass base holding the kerosene broke, and Michelle caught fire upon impact.

With his last gasp of breath, Alex pushed her backward, sending her tumbling down the steps, lighting the way as she fell. Each step in its turn lit from the spilled kerosene, and Alex knew that they had just a few minutes before the smoke and fire consumed them all.

That's when he heard the shouting from below them.

On the ground, a wave of men came rushing in at the base of the lighthouse. Alex leaned over the edge and saw them beating at the flames on Michelle, trying to stop the fire. The stairs were easier to extinguish, since they'd gotten less fuel on them than the killer had. They were all easily extinguished with a blanket, and the last thing that Alex remembered was looking up at Elise and saying, "I'm sorry."

And then his entire world went black.

Chapter 20

Alex awoke in a hospital room, but he didn't see the cream-colored walls, the tiled ceiling, or the curtains that surrounded him.

All he saw was Elise.

He tried to talk, but he couldn't manage more than a grunt.

Elise looked at him, tears in her eyes, and she smiled so brightly he thought his heart would explode.

"Sore," he managed to say as she delicately hugged him. "Need water."

She gave him a sip, then another, and his throat felt instantly better.

The next thing that he asked her was, "Are you okay?"

"Fortunately my head's thicker than Michelle counted on," Elise said. "Plus, my hair is so thick that it managed to soften most of the blow. If I'd had short hair, I would have probably been dead."

"I like it long," he managed to say with a slight grin. "Did she make it?" Alex asked.

"She's in the burn ward," was all that Elise would say.

Alex could see that she was distressed by what she'd been forced to do, but he was glad that she'd done it.

"Elise, you saved us."

She shook her head. "Not a chance. You took a knife in the stomach that was meant for me, and then you distracted her long enough for me in the end so I could hit her with that lantern."

"We saved each other, then," he said. He was so very tired, but he needed to have this conversation with her before he lost consciousness again.

"I can live with that if you can," Elise said. She

touched his shoulder and said, "You'll be okay soon. She didn't do as much damage as they first thought, and as soon as you got a transfusion, your vital signs perked right up." Elise brushed a bit of hair out of his eyes and said, "It looks like you're going to have to live up to your end of the bargain after all."

"What bargain?" he asked, his head still swirling from what had happened.

Elise looked shattered by his reaction. Why was she acting that way? Then it all came flooding back to him. "Hey, we're getting married," he finally managed to say with a smile.

"If you still want to," she answered softly.

"Just try to stop me," Alex replied, and without thinking, Elise started to hug him.

He pulled back from the pain, and she looked at him lovingly. "Sorry. I wasn't sure you'd still want to marry me. Alex, I won't hold you to it. You proposed when you thought we were both going to die. It's not fair to make you follow through on something you said when you thought that we were both about to die."

"No one can make me do anything I don't want to. Go through my luggage when you leave here. I've had an engagement ring forever, and I've just been waiting for the right time to ask you. I want this more than you know."

"Not as much as I do. You know, it's amazing what Michelle was willing to do just for money. I hope it never has a hold on me that way."

Alex smiled at her. "You're marrying an innkeeper. Being rich won't ever be a problem for you, Elise."

She kissed him again and then said, "That's where you're wrong. We're rich, Alex, in every way that counts but a bank balance or a stock portfolio."

He was about to reply when they both heard a familiar bellowing voice coming from the hallway. "He isn't my brother by birth, but he's still my family. Now, if you don't move out of the way, I'm going to move you."

"You'd better do what he says. He means it," another familiar voice said.

"It's Mor and Emma," Alex said with a smile.

Elise nodded. "I figured they'd be here soon. I called them as soon as you went into surgery. Now, I'd better go let them in before Mor breaks the door down."

"I can't wait to tell him the good news," Alex said.

"Sorry, but you're too late," Elise answered with a laugh. "It was the first thing out of my mouth the second I called them."

As Elise went out to clear the way for their friends, Alex let his mind drift away. It had taken a crisis to bring them the last step together, and Alex knew that nothing short of the end of the world would ever keep them apart again.

To learn more about Tim Myers's novels, please visit www.timmyersfiction.com.

Books by Tim Myers

Lighthouse Mystery Series
Innkeeping with Murder
Reservations for Murder
Murder Checks Inn
Room for Murder
Booked for Murder
Key to Murder
Ring for Murder

Candlemaking Series
At Wick's End
Snuffed Out
Death Waxed Over
A Flicker of Doubt
Waxing Moon

Soapmaking Series
Dead Men Don't Lye
A Pour Way to Dye
A Mold for Murder

Cardmaking Series
Invitation to Murder
Deadly Greetings
Murder and Salutations

Slow Cooker Mysteries
Slow Cooked Murder
Simmering Death

Standalone Cozy Mysteries
A Family of Strangers
Coventry
Volunteer for Murder

Paranormal Adult

Werewolf PI
Zombie PI

Romantic Fantasy
The Fairy Godfather

Suspense
Caved In
Cornered
Hunted
Iced
Trapped

Short Story Collections
A Touch of Romance
Beauty Times 3
Can You Guess What's Next? Vol. 1
Can You Guess What's Next? Vol. 2
Crimes with a Twist
Dark Shots
Dark Sips of Mystery
Did You Solve the Crime? Vol. 1
Did You Solve the Crime? Vol. 2
Did You Solve the Crime? Vol. 3
Hidden Messages
Long Shots
Marriage Can Be Murder
Money Mysteries
Murder Is a Special Occasion
Murder Nine to Five
Pet Mysteries
Repeat Performances
Senior Sleuths Again
Senior Sleuths Times 3
Turning the Tables

Middle-Grade Readers
Book of Time and Ben Franklin

Book of Time and Thomas Edison
Book of Time and Archimedes
Crispin Livingston Hughes, Boy Inventor
Emma's Emerald Mine
Lost in Monet's Garden
Lost in Picasso's Cubes

Young Adult Mysteries
Lightning Ridge
Rebuilding My Life
Tackling the Truth
Voltini

Young Adult Sci-Fi & Fantasy
Paranormal Kids
Paranormal Camp
Wizard's School Year 1: The Wizard's Secret
Wizard's School Year 2: The Killing Crystal

Books by Tim Myers writing as Chris Cavender

Pizza Mystery Series
A Slice of Murder
Thin Crust Killers
Pepperoni Pizza Can Be Murder
A Pizza to Die For
Rest in Pizza
Killer Crust
The Missing Dough

Books by Tim Myers writing as Casey Mayes

Mystery by the Numbers
A Deadly Row
A Killer Column
A Grid for Murder